Hemlock Hill Hideaway

Books by Carrie Bender

Miriam's Journal Series

A Fruitful Vine
A Winding Path
A Joyous Heart
A Treasured Friendship
A Golden Sunbeam
Miriam's Cookbook

WHISPERING BROOK SERIES

Whispering Brook Farm
Summerville Days
Chestnut Ridge Acres
Hemlock Hill Hideaway

Dora's Diary Series

Birch Hollow Schoolmarm
Lilac Blossom Time

Hemlock Hill Hideaway

Carrie Bender

Herald
Press

Scottdale, Pennsylvania
Waterloo, Ontario

Library of Congress Cataloging-in-Publication Data
Bender, Carrie, date.
Hemlock Hill Hideaway / Carrie Bender
p. cm.—(Whispering Brook series ; 4)
Summary: When the elder Petersheims buy a farm for young Omar, his sister comes to keep house for him, and together they make a new home for the mischievous Dannie.
ISBN 0-8361-9128-5
[1. Amish—Fiction. 2. Family life—Fiction. 3. Farm life—Fiction.]
I. Title
PZ7.B43136 HE 2000 99-055154
[Fic]—dc21

The paper used in this publication is recycled and meets the minimum requirements of American National Standard for Information Sciences—Permanence of Paper for Printed Library Materials, ANSI Z39.48-1984.

Note: This story is fiction, but true to Amish life. Any resemblance to persons living or dead is coincidental.

Library of Congress Catalog Number: 99-055154
International Standard Book Number: 0-8361-9128-5
Printed in the United States of America
Cover art and illustrations by Joy Dunn Keenan
Book design by Sandra Johnson

09 08 07 06 05 04 03 02 01 00 10 9 8 7 6 5 4 3 2 1

To order or request information, please call
1-800-759-4447 (individuals); 1-800-245-7894 (trade).
Website: www.mph.org

Contents

1

Surprise!

NANCY Petersheim swung her bonnet round and round by its strings as she trudged homeward through the field lane. The fragrant, woodsy autumn breeze was dancing around her, with mellow hazy sunshine all around. Nancy was returning home after a busy morning of helping a neighbor.

She glanced with pleasure at the bare cornfields on either side of the lane, glad that the corn was harvested and the silos filled for another year. Now she could see way over to the Vaneski mansion on one side, and to Covered Bridge Road on the other.

Her eyes traveled fondly over dear Whispering Brook Farm. The beloved old sandstone farmhouse stood firm. So did the cozy old barn, where cute kittens romped and played, pigeons cooed peacefully from the rafters, and horses whinnied for their feed.

The buildings were surrounded by the dear, familiar fields and trees. Nancy knew and loved every dell and slope, every wooded knob and shady glen of the place.

There was the friendly old orchard with its gnarled apple trees, where the Petersheim children had spent many an evening playing. The fir grove threw its mysterious shadows. To the east was the familiar row of Lombardy poplars, and beside the barn was the old maple tree. She had loved to climb its lofty branches and crawl into her leafy secret perch.

The enchanting meadow, with Whispering Brook flowing through it, was still her favorite. When she was younger, she had once delighted in naming every path and even the trees. Nancy sighed. She knew it was time to put away such childish doings. After all, in a few years she would already be *rumschpringing!* (running around with the youths).

Nancy heard the peal of the dinner bell and quickened her steps. She squinted her eyes against the bright sunshine, watching as Omar drove Belle and Bo, hitched to a wagonload of corn. The wagon had come in from the south field, where a few big orange pumpkins still dotted the slope.

Her brother guided the big workhorses under the forebay (barn overhang) to unhitch, while a few lively kittens nimbly scampered away from the big clopping feet. They had heard the dinner bell, too.

Nancy looked again, blinking in surprise. Was that

Steven on the wagon with Omar? But, no, it couldn't be! Steven was the *Gnecht* (hired man) for Joe and Arie on the Chestnut Ridge farm, several hours away by van, in the Summerville area.

She began to run, her bonnet flapping wildly behind her. Nancy reached the barn just as Steven—yes, it was Steven!—jumped off the wagon, grinning broadly at her.

"*Wu kummst du bei* (where do you come from)?" Nancy cried in amazement. "Are Joe and Arie here, too?"

"Sure are," he replied, "and Jacob and Mary, too. We decided to surprise you all."

"Hurrah!" Nancy made a dash for the house, not caring that a few minutes ago she was considering herself fairly grown up, prim, and proper. The kitchen door flew open, and little Nancy Ann came trotting out to meet her. Nancy caught her niece up in a big bear hug. "My, it's so good to see you again, Nancy Ann!"

"Aunt Nancy, Aunt Nancy!" the little girl cried over and over.

Mary met Nancy at the door. "*Wie geht's* (how is it going)?" Nancy greeted her with shining eyes. She shook hands with her sister Mary and sister-in-law Arie. In the *Sitzschtubb* (sitting room), Dad was visiting with Joe and Jacob.

"What a delightful surprise!" Nancy exclaimed. "Why didn't you tell us you were coming?"

"We only found out yesterday that there was room for us in the vanload," Mary told her. "Surprises like this are nice, too, aren't they?"

"*Ya*, they certainly are!" Nancy agreed. She put Nancy Ann on the high stool at the end of the table and looked at the bounteous table. It had been stretched out and extra leaves put in for the occasion.

What a meal she saw! There was a big platter of juicy ham balls, steaming mashed potatoes, creamed corn, homemade noodles, and cabbage slaw. Slices of fresh, light bread and pats of golden butter—everything homemade, of course—with shimmering, molded raspberry jelly to put on top.

"Tell the men that dinner is ready," said Mom. Arie had finished filling the water glasses, and the boys were washing up at the water pump.

"This sure is a nice surprise, having the whole family together like this." Dad beamed as he took his place at the head of the table. "It doesn't happen so often anymore."

"It's a rare treat," Mom agreed. "But it would be even more rare if the children lived out of state."

The family bowed their heads to ask the blessing. Nancy's heart filled with joyful thanksgiving at having all the family together once again. *Even Mammi (Grandma) is here,* she thought, *though we sure do miss Daadi (Grandpa).*

The scholars had come home from school for lunch, too. Yes, Grandpa was gone, but new ones were entering the family, such as Nancy Ann. Maybe, just maybe, Joe and Arie would have a surprise for them, come spring.

Jacob spoke up. "We had good reason for hoping

we'd have the chance to come here today. There's a farm coming up for sale next to ours. The buildings are a half-mile north of us. *Daed* (Dad), we thought you might be interested in buying it before someone else does.

"It has nearly a hundred acres of nice, fairly level land, and the buildings are in good shape." Jacob waited to hear what Dad would have to say.

Dad paused, his spoonful of jelly in midair.

"You'll be needing a farm for Omar before too long," Joe said. "If the price is reasonable and—"

"Does the farm have a name?" Nancy interrupted eagerly.

Jacob chuckled. "You would be the one to ask that. No, it doesn't, but you can give it one. Beyond the fields, there's a wooded knob on the north side of the farm that's even bigger than Joe's chestnut ridge. It has a lot of hemlocks and pines of all sorts, and it's a good place to gather hickory nuts. Call it Hickory Hill Farm if you wish."

Nancy's eyes grew dreamy. "If it has hemlocks, I'll call it Hemlock Hill Farm—no, Hemlock Hill Homestead would be better, just the thing!"

"Three cheers!" Susie agreed "But . . . a farm for Omar? He doesn't even have an *Aldi* (girlfriend) yet. I wish he would."

"Hmph, I wouldn't worry about that," Steven cut in. "Just wait and see. I have a feeling that when the right one comes along, he won't fiddle around for long."

Omar gave him a withering look. "Even a bachelor needs land and buildings, if he wants to farm."

"Ha," Henry scoffed. "I never heard of anyone being a bachelor before he was twenty-one."

Omar turned to his dad. "I'm all for it, Daed, if Nancy comes and keeps house for me." His voice was full of barely controlled excitement. Nancy just sat there openmouthed, staring at him.

Dad finished spreading jelly on his bread and cleared his throat. "You say the price is right?" He and his sons were soon in a lively discussion about what would be a fair price.

Mary turned to her mother. "Oh, *Mamm*, I do hope you folks can buy it. To have another one of the family so close, that would be almost too good to be true. And we need some more young people at Summerville."

"Now wait a minute," Nancy sputtered. "I didn't know I was going to be involved in this. I think I'm still tied to Mamm's apron strings.

"Oh, I'll come and work for you sisters whenever you have a new baby, and that should be good enough. I won't promise to keep house for anybody, not even for Omar."

Nancy was quite sure that she would not. However, she didn't know that, come spring, she would indeed be moving to Summerville on the newly named Hemlock Hill Homestead—as Omar's housekeeper.

2

Hemlock Hill

LESS than a week later, the Petersheim family was in a van and headed for Summerville, to look at the farm for sale. Everyone had wanted to go along, and Dad had said jovially, "The more the merrier. Besides, the more people to help us make up our mind, the better. Isn't that so, Omar?"

Omar grinned. "My mind's already made up, Daed. But sure, let them all come."

It was an exciting day for the family, especially for Omar. Nancy was caught up in the excitement, too. By now, she had halfway accepted the possibility of moving to Summerville as being a real adventure.

Besides, it might not be for long. She agreed with Steven that Omar would likely soon find himself an

Aldi and get married. Then she would be free to come home.

"It will even be exciting while it lasts," she told herself. "I should be able to make myself at home there, with Mary so close, and my old friend Sally. She and her brother Andrew are a lively set. All that should keep me from getting homesick."

The van finally turned into the straight, tree-lined lane at the farm. Nancy eagerly tried to take in everything at once: the white-plastered stone house and the big bank barn, the wind wheel (windmill) turning in the breeze, and the wide fields. Beyond them was the mountain knob on the north that she had already named Hemlock Hill.

"Look," Lydia squealed. "There's a swing set in the yard, and big shade trees."

"See that big pond out back?" Henry said admiringly. "Why, it's almost like a lake. What fun we could have swimming in it and skating on it."

"Look at all those pine trees back of the house," Susie exclaimed. "It's sure pretty."

"From the looks of things, it might be in much better shape than Joe's farm was," Dad commented. "We wouldn't have as much work to fix things up."

"Let's hope we can get in, to see inside the house," Mom declared. "I do hope it's fairly clean. I wouldn't want another one like Joe and Arie's. That took a lot of cleaning up."

The front door was locked, but the back door squeaked open. "It's clean," Nancy said with relief. "Hey, just look at that big fireplace."

She went into the next room. "And here's another. A fireplace in every room!"

"The linoleum's in good shape, too," Mom noted. "So glad it's not stained and musty wall-to-wall carpet."

The back door squeaked open again. "Well, well, just look who's coming here!" Nancy cried, in astonishment.

"Sally Fisher, *wu kummst du bei* (where do you come from)?"

Sally laughed merrily at Nancy's question. "When we saw you folks drive in, we just couldn't stay away, Andrew and I. Oh, we're hoping so much you'll buy this farm. That would be a dream come true!"

"Are you sure your family isn't interested in this farm?" Mom asked Sally. "We don't want to cause bad feelings if—"

"Oh no," Sally said quickly. "Dad only has one boy, and he intends to pass on the harness shop to him. Oh, you just must buy this farm. Old Man Magee farmed here, and he was really a grouch. He never let us skate on his big pond. Imagine all the skating parties we could have if you buy it."

Just then Andrew and Omar came in the back door and overheard Sally's plans. "Don't count your chicks before they're hatched," Omar cautioned. "If we act too eager, the real estate man may up his price, and the deal might fall through."

Andrew added, "If that happens, trying to cheer Sally up would be mighty difficult."

"Huh!" Sally retorted. "You should have seen

Andrew when he saw you people drive in here. Talk about being excited!"

"Just look at this." Nancy opened a door under the kitchen counter. "A nearly brand-new dishwasher. Wow, won't this be handy!"

Susie gazed enviously at the shiny appliance. "Just think, you won't have to wash stacks and stacks of dishes ever again!"

"Now, now," Mom chided. "You know we'll turn off the electricity. We don't want to use anything that's against the *Ordnung* (church rules). Come on, children. I think it's time we start for Jacob's place now. Mary will have dinner ready shortly. Sally and Andrew, I'm sure you are welcome to have dinner there, too."

"Thanks, but no thanks." Sally declined for them both. "I have a stew simmering on the stove, and we have to wait on our shop customers while Mom and Dad eat. I might be over this afternoon, though."

"Please do come." Nancy smiled. "I'd like to get caught up on all the doings of the Summerville youngsters."

"Let's hope those papers are all signed before you leave here," Sally said fervently. "Ah, how I hope, how I hope!"

Nancy stifled a giggle. She had forgotten how dramatic Sally could be.

• • •

At the dinner table at Jacobs' place, Nancy noticed a *fremm* (strange) young boy seated on the bench with her brothers. Nancy had never seen him before, not even at church services here in Summerville. He was wearing a plain solid-color shirt and homemade broadfall pants with wide suspenders, just like the other boys. His eyes were blue, and a thatch of blonde hair fell across his forehead.

I wonder who he is, Nancy mused. *Maybe one of Jacob's relatives from another district.*

"Pass the potatoes, Dannie," Jacob said in English to the boy.

So his name is Dannie. I wonder what his last name is. He appeared to be about eleven years old and small for his age. Nancy thought she detected a look of hurt or even a bit of defiance in his eyes. Who could it be?

Not till the menfolk had left the table and gone back outside did Mary explain. "The past few weeks, Dannie has been our community's foster child. He was an only child, and his mother died five years ago. Ever since, he and his dad lived alone. Then about six weeks ago, his dad up and left him, actually abandoned him and went out into loose living.

"As a result, the poor boy has turned into a problem child. He was staying with his uncle and family until he became too hard to handle there. Now he's been taking turns in staying with different Amish families here at Summerville. He gets along with others for a while at each place, until the newness wears off, and then he's back to his old tricks. He's said to be the most mischievous boy ever."

Mary sighed. "This is only the second day he's staying with us, and I'm hoping for the best. I just wish you could arrange to take him home with you. We all know how good Daed is with boys, with all the wisdom and patience he has."

Mom nodded thoughtfully. "Where does he go to school?" she wondered.

Mary sighed again. "He was suspended from public school just after his dad left. The school board here at our Amish school didn't really want to take him, but that's where he has been going. He has played hooky several times. And the pranks he has played! *Ach mei!* (oh, my)."

"Hmmm." Mom was thinking things over. "We have a real good teacher at our district's Amish school back home, one with years of experience. Your teacher here is in her first year of teaching, isn't she?"

"Yes, and it's quite a challenge for her to handle such a case," Mary said sadly. "I don't know what will happen yet. It's disrupting the whole school. Please talk to Daed about taking Dannie to stay with you. Or maybe Jacob already has."

"We'll think it over," Mom promised, when the van had come to pick up the family and they were getting ready to leave. "It might not be easy to have Dannie transferred to yet another school. But we'll do what we can to help you, no matter what we decide."

The good-byes were said, and Nancy plopped into the backseat of the van and leaned back. *What an eventful day,* she thought. They had seen the

Hemlock Hill Homestead for the first time, and she had enjoyed a jolly afternoon with Sally. Then they heard the news that the papers were all signed for the farm, and the date was set for taking possession of it.

When Omar got in, Nancy could tell that he was on cloud nine. "Full steam ahead!" he bantered jubilantly, winking at Nancy. "Are you ready?"

"Full steam ahead," Nancy mimicked. "Already you're sounding like Andrew."

Oh, well, she mused, *maybe they'll be good for each other. Omar needed some livening up, and Andrew needed some toning down. Yes, and Sally and I will probably be good for each other, too.*

3

The Crow

SIX weeks later, on Thanksgiving Day, the whole family once more got together, this time with Joe and Arie at Chestnut Ridge Acres. They had a turkey dinner with all the trimmings. It was a mild, balmy day, and the young people spent the afternoon hiking on the Chestnut Ridge.

Dannie was along, too. Arrangements had been made for him to travel home with the Petersheim family and stay at Whispering Brook Farm. When the boys came trooping down from the top of the ridge, Dannie was cradling a young crow in his arms. His blue eyes were bright with excitement.

"Get a box," he told Steven. "I'm going to take this crow with me. I think he was attacked by a hawk a while ago and couldn't get around to find himself enough to eat. He's half dead."

"You'd better ask Daed if you may," Susie cautioned. "And the driver might not like to take a smelly crow in his van."

Dannie's eyes narrowed. "I said I'm taking it along!" Defiance shone out of his eyes, as if daring her to cross him. "I'll give it a bath when we get there."

"Hush," Nancy whispered, after taking Susie aside. "It will never do for us to contradict him. And it might be good for him to have something to look after. I just hope it won't die for him."

"But what if it has lice?" Susie wrinkled her nose. "That bird gives me the creeps."

Dad had instructed the boys to try to overlook Dannie's anger and to be friendly to him. "Above all, be sure never to tease him. That way, the hurts within can heal, and we might draw out the better side of him."

Now Omar promised Dannie, "You can keep the crow in a box behind the kitchen stove until he's better. And we have plenty of mash for him, out in the chicken house."

When Mom saw the sorry-looking bird as she got into the van, she raised her eyebrows questioningly at Dad. He merely nodded and said to her in a low voice, "Taking it away from him would only make him sullen."

The bird lay quietly all the way home, barely breathing.

Poor thing, Nancy thought sadly. *When the crow*

dies, he'll be hurt all over again. She closed her eyes and murmured, "Please, God, let the crow live for Dannie's sake. He badly needs something to love."

At home that evening, Dannie barely touched his supper. He was absorbed with caring for the pet crow. Dannie insisted on sleeping on the settee, in the kitchen near the stove. On the wood chest behind the stove, the crow was nested in the box, on a soft cloth.

"If tender loving care can save the crow, it sure will live," Dad told Mom at bedtime, amazed at how important the bird seemed to Dannie. "If it does die, we'll see what we can do about getting him some bunnies or a puppy. I believe he has a soft spot in his heart for small, helpless animals."

"Yes," Mom agreed. "I don't think he's as bad-natured as some seem to think."

"What will you name your crow?" Lydia asked shyly, watching as Dannie tenderly wrapped it in the soft cloth.

Dannie shrugged. "I thought Silas would be nice." He swallowed hard. Silas was his dad's name.

• • •

To the amazement of all, the crow improved rapidly. He was soon hopping around the kitchen, especially at mealtimes, and screeching for tidbits to be thrown to him. Dannie had adjusted well to starting at a new school and had gotten into no bad mischief, if the family didn't count choking a rooster. Of course, he hadn't meant to do it.

Dannie and Lydia were sweeping the feed alley in the cow stable, and he had seen Lassie pounce upon a mouse and hold it down with his paws. For some reason, Dannie did not like Lassie, and the feeling was mutual. He grabbed a milk stool and chased Lassie off. Dannie managed to grab the mouse before it ran off, then tossed it to the big leghorn rooster, scratching for insects in the barnyard.

With one fell swoop, the rooster caught the mouse and gobbled it up. Uh, oh! He choked and wheezed, but the mouse would neither go down nor come up. In a few minutes, the rooster fell over. Dannie stared at it, dumbfounded.

"Why Dannie, look what you've done!" Lydia gasped. "It's dead."

Dannie dropped his broom and rushed out of the cow stable. He made a beeline for the kitchen, picked up Silas the crow, and was seen heading across the meadow toward Whispering Brook.

Lydia watched him go, then picked up the limp rooster, took it to Dad, and told him what had happened. Dad chopped off its head and helped Lydia pluck the feathers. Mom butchered the big rooster, stuffed it with bread filling, and popped it into the big range oven.

That evening, when supper was nearly ready, Dannie and the crow were still nowhere to be found. Dad sent Omar to look for him.

Omar trudged down through the meadow, glad for the chance to look for signs of wildlife. Deer season would open next week, and he had plans to hunt

with Andrew on Hemlock Hill on his farm. He was eager to find out how plentiful the deer actually were there.

Following Dannie's tracks in the light dusting of snow, he saw a cottontail rabbit bound away and spotted a few muskrat tracks. But the wildlife was not as abundant here as it was at Summerville. He could hardly wait to hunt there.

A few minutes later, he spied the blue of Dannie's coat on the other side of a log. *Poor boy,* Omar thought. *I must reassure him that it wasn't his fault. We had been planning to butcher that rooster at Christmastime anyway.*

He paused to listen, hearing Dannie say something in a crooning voice to the crow. "Dad will come back for me, Silas, I just know it. Will you be my friend till he comes?"

Listening to him, Omar's eyes misted over. He remembered how abandoned and rejected he had felt years ago when he thought he was being accused of setting a building afire. His heart went out in pity to the boy.

"Come, Dannie boy," he called. "Supper's ready. And thanks to you, we're having roasted rooster and filling."

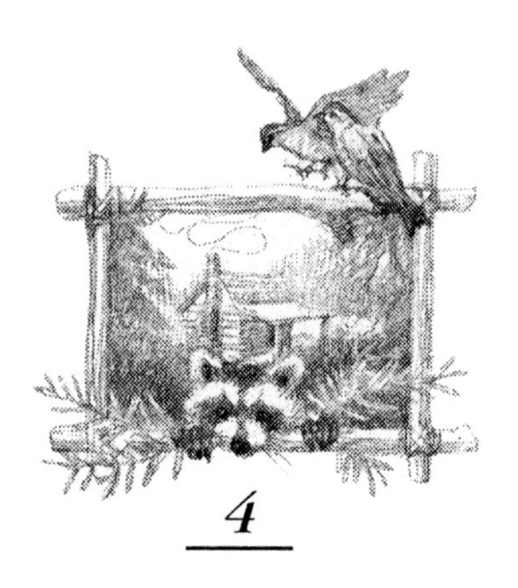

4

Pranks

SILAS the crow was learning to talk and stirring up all kinds of mischief. Dannie had gotten into a bit of mischief himself.

One Saturday, the boys were out in the barn, currying the buggy horses so they would be ready to take the family to church the next day. Dannie was trying his hand at currying Omar's horse, Beauty, with the stiff-bristled currycomb, when a sudden gleam of mischief flashed into his eyes.

He continued brushing Beauty's glossy back, waiting till the horse raised his tail slightly. Then with a guilty glance at Omar, quick as a flash Dannie stuck the stiff brush under the horse's tail!

In less time than it takes to tell, the tail was

clamped down ever so tightly on the currycomb. Whew! The poor frightened horse took a terrific lunge forward, then sideways, and the dance was on.

It was impossible for Omar to get the brush out, and the nearly wild Beauty bucked and tore around so badly that Dannie flew into a corner. Omar was nearly knocked off his feet. But that irritating brush was still there, under Beauty's tail.

Nancy was in the cow stable, milking her last cow. She heard the terrible commotion and hurried off to find Dad, who was feeding the steers. She was sure that the big horse had gone mad.

Dad came on the run. "Whoa, Beauty," he commanded, in his strong voice. But Beauty was too distracted by the brush that was driving him crazy and paid no heed. Dad could not get the brush either. He grabbed the horse twitch from its hook and tried to fasten it to Beauty's nose. But the horse was still too wild and he couldn't attach the twitch.

Finally Dad pushed a sheet of plywood beside the horse to protect him from being kicked. With Omar's help, he managed to remove the irksome brush. In great relief, Beauty stood there, trembling. Dad was rubbing his sore arm, not sure whether he had been kicked or rammed. Dannie had disappeared quickly from the stable and was nowhere to be found.

"*Unvergleichlich!* (weird)," Dad muttered. "I suppose it was Dannie who did it."

Omar nodded, trying not to laugh. Henry had doubled over with laughter and quickly left the stable so Dad wouldn't see him.

Now that the danger was over, it was rather funny. But Dad, whose arm was smarting badly, couldn't see it that way. "The boy will have to be punished," he said. "He must learn that we treat our animals kindly on this farm."

Omar nodded. "That's true. But he probably thought it would just be a harmless prank, never realizing how serious the consequences could be."

"Maybe so," Dad agreed. "Since this is his first serious offense, I guess I can let him off with a lecture."

Then there was the case of the lost deer meat. When Omar came home from Hemlock Hill with a big, stately ten-point buck, his first one, Dannie was as excited as the other boys. Eagerly he helped hang the prize trophy on a limb of the big maple tree in the barnyard. They all admired it there for a few days while it was aging in the cold air, so it would be more tender.

Omar had decided to tackle the job of processing the deer himself, rather than having it sent to the butcher shop to be done. So the big kettles and knives were brought out after school one day, and they took the buck down from the tree limb. With Henry's and Dannie's help, the job was done by evening. The big tub of cut-up meat was set on the porch, where it was cold, to be made into hamburger after supper.

The task of cleaning up was left to the girls, and the boys went out to the barn to start the chores. Dannie got his coat and cap and went out on the back porch to take another satisfying look at the good meat. As soon as supper was over, they would set up the meat grinders, and he was eager to help. Butchering was a lot of fun, and he had never tasted venison before!

Mom was at the stove, rolling slices of deer liver in flour and frying it in butter, adding salt and pepper. Mmmm! She glanced out the window and saw Dannie standing there, surveying the meat with an air of satisfaction. Mom rejoiced that he had adjusted to their family so well. Things were going smoothly at school, too.

She went to the cellar for potatoes to peel, and Dannie ran off to the barn to help with the chores. As soon as the table was cleared after supper, Omar set up the meat grinder and went to bring in the tub of meat. With a cry of dismay, he saw that the tub was empty. Omar called out, "Dannie, what did you do with the deer meat?"

Dannie sprang up from the bench. "Nothing! What happened?" The puzzled look on his face seemed genuine.

"It's gone!" Omar cried indignantly. "Tell me where it is, and *mach schnell* (hurry up)."

"I don't know, honest I don't! Why do you always blame me?" Dannie was frightened. Everyone knew he had been the last one out on the back porch where the meat had been. He grabbed his coat and cap, dived under the table to where his pet crow was picking around for crumbs, and grabbed him. Before anyone could stop him, he darted out the door and headed for the meadow.

Tears coursed down over Dannie's cheeks.

"Nobody loves me!" he cried. "They blame me for everything that happens. I hate them all."

Seeing the kitchen door opening and Omar coming out, Dannie quickly dived behind a bush "Dannie, Dannie, come back!" Omar called.

Dannie stayed as still as he could and heard the sound of Omar's voice echoing back from the hills. He heard Omar say, "He's gone," and saw him go back into the house.

"*Ach mei* (oh, my)," Mom lamented. "Maybe Lassie took the meat. Let's hunt for it, before we decide Dannie took it."

They searched, and sure enough, there in the west yard, they saw Lassie at Nancy's large round flowerbed with the miniature wind wheel. Decorative rocks marked a ring around the flowerbed. Lassie was sniffing and digging in the loose soft mushroom mulch of the bed.

Dannie was watching from behind the bush. He saw them chase Lassie away and pick up the meat from the flowerbed, piece by piece. He grinned to himself. This was funny, now that his name was cleared. He laughed out loud. He watched as Omar pumped water over the meat and rinsed it again and again. Now he knew he could go in and help crank the meat grinder after all.

Omar apologized to Dannie. But he never quite forgave Lassie for spoiling the meat of his first deer. They rinsed the meat over and over to clean it, and worked hard to grind it. The boys wrapped it and took it to the freezer locker they rented at a food storage depot. Yet later they couldn't eat even one package of it, even after it was well cooked. It still tasted and smelled of the mulch.

When their neighbor heard what had happened, he warned Omar that if the meat tasted bad, it likely wasn't safe anyhow. He gave Omar a cut of meat from another deer he had gotten.

So Omar was consoled, and they all tried a sample of the venison.

5

Star

DAD had bought a new horse for Steven, a sixteen-hand (64-inch) tall bay standardbred trotter, with a white patch on his forehead. With Steven's permission, Nancy promptly named him Star.

He was just green broken and a bit skittish yet. The first time they took Star out, Omar and Steven hitched him to the two-wheeled breaking (training) cart. This cart was used for breaking in horses because it would not jacknife if an unruly horse turned too sharply. Dannie wanted to go along, too, but Omar told him to wait at the end of the lane till they came back. Then he could have a turn, too.

Down to the Covered Bridge Road they went, then turned around and headed back. All the way, Star was upheaded and warily eyeing every strange-looking post and bush, but didn't shy away from them. He didn't seem to mind the traffic at all.

When they came back to the end of the lane, Omar told Dannie to hop on, making room for him in the middle between Omar and Steven.

"Giddyup!" Dannie cried. "Let's get some speed!" Before Omar could stop him, he grabbed one of the reins in Steven's hand and slapped the horse's rump with it. Star jumped, then took off at a gallop. It was all Steven could do to get his horse under control.

A bunch of holstein cows were in a meadow right beside the road. It was too much for Star. He shied away from them, out into the middle of the pavement. A panel truck was coming their way and swerved to pass, with just a fraction of an inch to spare—so it seemed to Omar, who was sitting on that side.

"You'd better behave, or I'll dump you off right here!" Steven growled. "No more of that stuff."

Dannie obeyed, but a storm was brewing inside him. He hadn't seen the danger they were in and couldn't understand why what he had done was so bad. *Steven's just a bossy old fussbudget*, he thought angrily. *I'll get him back sometime. I'm sure Omar would even let me drive if Steven weren't with us.*

Star trotted along nicely for the next mile and a half. Then Steven slowed him to a walk and turned him into a long tree-lined lane that led to a farm. A sign on a fence post said SHADY LANE TACK SHOP.

"I'll be needing a new horse blanket for Star," Steven explained. "While I'm here, I'll order a new harness for him, too." He tied Star at the tie railing by the barn. Dannie followed Steven and Omar into the shop.

A boy was sweeping some shavings into a pile with a big push broom. He was a bit younger than Dannie and smiled at him. "Hi!" he said.

Dannie had seen him at church but couldn't remember his name. He soon learned that it was Abie. He was a friendly, outgoing boy, and before long they were chatting away like old friends.

"You ought to come outside and see Steven's new horse," Dannie urged. "He just got him today, and this is the first time we hitched him. Let's go."

Abie dropped his broom. "Can he go fast?" He followed Dannie out the door.

Dannie chortled. "I'm sure he could, but Steven's so bossy, and he just drove along like a poky old grandmother. I wish I could drive him by myself. Then we would really fly!"

A bright idea suddenly entered his mind. "Say, Abie, here's our chance!" Dannie cried in high glee. "We two can take him for a little spin! Let's go!"

Abie shook his head. "No way!" he declared, backing away, his eyes big with disbelief. "I know better than that."

"Pooh! You're scared," Dannie scoffed. "You're a chicken if you don't *mach schnell* (hurry up), *schpring uff* (jump on), and take the reins while I untie the rope." By this time, the *englisch* (non-Amish) boy Dannie had picked up a few words of Pennsylvania German and liked to show them off.

Dannie jerked the tie rope loose and unsnapped it. Star lunged backward in fright. Seeing that the horse was about to take off, Abie sprang forward and caught him by the bridle. Dannie was on the cart now and had the reins. "Giddyup!" he yelled, slapping the reins down hard on Star's back.

With a bound that nearly jolted Abie off his feet, Star was off, heading out the lane, with Dannie on the cart. Badly frightened for Dannie, Abie ran into the tack shop, shouting the bad news to Omar and Steven.

On the cart, Dannie was hanging onto the reins for dear life. He pulled them with all his might, shouting "WHOA, WHOA" to the galloping horse. At the end of the lane, Star turned out onto the road. The cart whirled around the corner on one wheel, nearly overturning. If traffic had been coming just then, they would have been in big trouble.

Dannie, clinging to the lines, managed to keep from falling off. He had been wishing for speed, and he got his fill! Star had been a racehorse and had just come off the track a few weeks earlier. Now, with not much pull on the bit, with his mane and tail flying in the wind, Star streaked down the road at breakneck speed.

This time Dannie was really frightened, knowing he had no control over the horse. The wind stung his face, and tears streamed down his cheeks. Frantically he tugged on the reins, but Star paid no heed. He was wild and free, a thing of grace and beauty, running faster and faster. Trees and houses flashed by. Dannie was dimly aware of traffic pulling off the road to let him pass.

Back at the tack shop, Omar and Steven ran outside and watched with growing dismay as Star and Dannie disappeared from sight at a dangerous speed. Abie's dad quickly offered to hitch his horse to the *Dachwaggeli* (roofed carriage) so the boys could try to follow the runaway. In a few minutes they were off, urging the older carriage horse on at his fastest pace.

Meanwhile, Dannie was growing increasingly terrified. He was debating whether to jump off, but fear held him back. Somehow he sensed that, at such a speed, jumping might be more dangerous than staying on the cart. Just ahead, a T intersection was coming up quickly. Dannie knew the horse was going too fast to make a turn to right or left. What would happen?

Straight ahead was a plowed field. Star leaped up over a low bank, nearly tossing Dannie off the cart in the big bump, then surged ahead, his powerful muscles rippling and surging. Traveling here was much harder than on the road. Dannie and the cart bounced up and down on the frozen ruts. Finally he let go of the reins and hung onto the cart, to keep from being thrown off.

After a few rounds through the field, Star got tired of it and slowed down of his own accord. When Omar and Steven caught up with them a short time later, Steven was able to catch Star with no trouble at all, much to the boy's relief.

"Well, Dannie," Omar said, "I guess you've learned your lesson, haven't you?"

Dannie nodded. "I-I'm sorry," he said in a small voice. "I just wanted to have a bit of fun. I'll never do it again."

All's well that ends well, Omar thought. He shuddered to imagine what might have happened.

6

Grief

THE winter passed quickly, with plenty of snow and ice to keep the young people from getting bored. They had lots of sledding and skating along with the usual work. The long winter evenings also provided time for reading and playing games, quilt and afghan making, and rug hooking or crocheting.

As spring approached, Omar and Nancy grew more and more excited about moving to Hemlock Hill Homestead! Time seemed to be going too slowly for them.

Dannie was happier than he had ever been since his dad abandoned him. He had received a new pair of skates for Christmas, and the whole family together had gotten a toboggan. Dannie was beginning to feel like part of this farm family. He had his good friend, Silas the crow, who patiently listened to all his troubles, wisely cocking his head to the side and keeping his counsel.

Then one day disaster struck. Dannie and Lassie had learned to tolerate each other, but the two never became real comrades.

Lassie and Silas absolutely despised each other. The only thing that kept Silas from succumbing to the dog's sharp jaws was the fact that he had wings. Often he took advantage of this to tease the dog mercilessly, flying low and pretending to attack him.

On several occasions, Silas actually nipped the dog's hindquarters, much to Dannie's amusement. This made Lassie furious, and she tried to keep an eye on the crow whenever he was close.

Of the few words Silas had learned to say, "Dannie" was the plainest and clearest. There was a strong bond between the boy and the crow.

One evening Dannie came into the feed entry of the barn and stumbled upon the tangle of feathers and innards that had once been his crow, now mangled. With a cry of anguish, he threw himself on the floor and howled piteously.

Everyone in the family took a turn at trying to comfort Dannie. They promised him a pup, or a pen of bunnies, or a lamb, or even a calf or a colt if he wanted one. But Dannie refused to be consoled or to listen to reason. He shouted, "I don't want any of those things."

No one had seen it happen; no one knew why or

how Lassie had finally managed to catch Silas. But the grisly deed was done, and the evidence was plain.

Dannie sobbed until he was exhausted. Then he comforted himself by planning revenge on the dog, and even on the whole family. *I will get even with them!* he resolved.

With this in mind, he at last agreed to go into the house after supper. He sat on the wood chest behind the stove, hoping he wouldn't be noticed. Company was there, a neighbor lady named Mrs. Goldfus. She was talkative, and Dannie soon forgot his plans for revenge while listening to her interesting story.

Mrs. Goldfus was saying, "My grandfather had a very adventurous time the summer he was nine years old. When he was ninety-five years old and bedfast, but with a clear mind, he talked so much about his experiences that I almost know them word for word. Someday I'd like to put it all in a book."

She paused as she rolled the stories over in her mind. Nancy pushed a bowl of popcorn toward her and said, with interest, "I sure would like to read your book. What happened to him?"

This was all the encouragement Mrs. Goldfus needed. Settling back into her rocker with a handful of popcorn, she began. "The summer of Grandpa's ninth year began with deep sorrow for him because his mother died of TB. His father couldn't keep the family together, so he and his brothers and sisters were parceled out to the relatives.

"Grandpa, whose name was Josh, was taken to live with an aunt and uncle. He remembered his dad loading his little youth bed on the back of a wagon pulled by two horses. Later he arrived at his uncle Joe's place.

"The uncle came out to the wagon and was about to unload Josh's things when his aunt Cass came running out of the house. She was scolding her husband, 'Don't unload that bed. Josh is not going to stay with us.' She yelled and protested until her face crumpled and she began to cry.

"His uncle Joe paid her no heed and proceeded calmly to unload the bed. 'We can't just turn the poor boy out,' he said. 'Where would he go?'

"With this, little Josh threw himself on the ground and began to sob. 'Why doesn't anyone want me?'

"He did not know that his aunt was really a good, kindhearted woman. But she was afraid the TB that took Josh's mother might be caught from the boy. In her mind's eye, she saw a row of coffins, with her children in them and maybe her husband as well.

"So Josh was wounded in his little heart by his aunt's unkind words and rejection. That night, when everyone was sleeping, he stuffed his few clothes and belongings into his pillowcase, sneaked out the door, and ran off into the night."

Dannie sat up straighter. This was getting to be interesting. He felt that he had something in common with Josh, and he wondered what Josh would do.

Nancy poured Mrs. Goldfus a glass of apple cider, and she continued. "Josh wandered until he was too tired to go further, then crept into an abandoned shed beside the road. He curled up on some straw and was soon fast asleep. This was in the summer, so it was not too cold." Mrs. Goldfus paused to sip some cider.

"In the morning Josh was awakened by someone yawning noisily on the other side of a thin partition. Then he heard movements and voices. Josh lay still, but he hadn't counted on the straw tickling his nose. Suddenly he sneezed loudly. In a wink the two round faces of a man and a woman appeared above the partition, staring at him in wide-eyed astonishment.

"The woman looked as if she couldn't believe her eyes. 'Bless you, boy! Where did you come from? You weren't here when we came in last night.'

"Josh was too frightened to answer, but the couple talked kindly to him and invited him to join them for breakfast. They built a small fire outside the shed and fried bacon and eggs.

"As they ate, the woman told him, 'We're Oscar and Susie Thompson, road walkers. We go from house to house, sometimes doing small jobs for people in exchange for the makings of a meal—things like these victuals here, and potatoes, other vegetables, and sometimes meat. Then we stop wherever it pleases us, build a fire, and cook us up a good stew. Do you care to join us?'

" 'Sure, come along,' Oscar welcomed him.

"Josh was happy to hike along with these kind, simple folks. He spent a few weeks with them in their hobo lifestyle. They slept in a different barn every night, after handing over their matches to the farmer.

"One night Susie became ill, and the old couple was taken to the poorhouse. Now Josh was on his own again. He knew it would never do for him to go alone from farm to farm, asking for meals. Josh grew hungry, wandering about the woods and meadows, hunting for berries, wild apples, or whatever.

"Finally his hunger forced Josh onto the road again. Here he met a kind family, Simon Brown and his wife and children."

Dannie had completely forgotten about Silas, so taken up was he with Mrs. Goldfus' story. He could hardly wait to hear the rest of the boy's adventures.

7

A Daring Plan

MRS. GOLDFUS reached for another handful of popcorn and continued the story about her grandfather Josh. "Traveling toward Josh came a rangy horse, hitched to an open spring wagon. A dark-skinned man and his wife sat on the front seat, and in the back were children of all sizes.

" 'Need a ride?' the man called, reining in his horse.

"Josh was weak from hunger, and he gratefully crowded on the back in the loose hay. The other children stared at him curiously. He wondered where these people were going.

"Josh didn't have long to wait. At the next farmhouse, the man pulled up at the back door. 'Hello, hello! My name is Simon. Can you spare a little ham for my children?' he called out to the farmer's wife, who answered his knock. 'And how about some hay for the horse?'

"The woman gave them no meat or ham, but she did hand them a basket of potatoes and turnips. At the next place, they received some wrinkled old apples, and Josh gratefully ate a few of them.

"When the man and his wife got out of the wagon, Josh noticed that she was limping. She did not seem to be in pain, so Josh decided the limp was from an old injury that had healed.

"At the next place Simon again asked for a piece of ham or *Schpeck* (bacon). The farmer told him, 'Well, I do have one rather old smoked ham I might let you have. That's, all I could spare—but only if you help me hoe the cornfield this afternoon.'

" 'Oh, fine!' the couple cried. 'We'll all help you. Just show us the hoes and the field. The children can pull weeds. We'll work for the ham, won't we, children?'

" 'Yes, yes!' they chorused.

"Josh went to the field with them. It was hot work, and they were glad for the water that the farmer's wife brought them. In the late afternoon, the farmer said, 'That's enough. Now you can have the ham.' He went to the basement and brought it out.

"Simon and his family were headed home with their prize. Finally he had the answer to his wish for a ham!

"The happy couple began to sing a little ditty, and the children joined in as the horse plodded homeward.

Happy are we all, happy are we all!
There's corn in the wagon and ham in the pot,
Taters in the skillet, piping hot,
Hay for the horse and sweets for the wife,
Mush for the chilluns, a jolly good life.
Happy are we all, happy are we all!

"Josh suddenly realized that if he stayed on the wagon, he would end up at their home. As much as his mouth watered for ham, he wasn't sure he wanted to become part of their family. When the horse slowed to make a turn, Josh jumped off the wagon and waved good-bye to the family.

"He walked back the way he had come. At the next farmhouse, he met another road walker, a stoop-shouldered old man coming out the lane. He saw him stash a fat packet of sandwiches into his big knapsack. Those thick slices of homemade bread had such a pull on Josh that he followed the man, who turned around and demanded, 'What do you want?'

" 'I'm awfully hungry,' Josh whimpered. 'Couldn't you spare me just one slice of the bread?' The tramp thought for a bit, then reached into his sack and tossed a slice of bread to the boy. He knew that boys of that size could be a terror for throwing stones.

"The bread was delicious but only seemed to further whet his appetite. Josh kept following the old man, walking about ten feet behind him and hoping he would also stop at the next farmhouse. He did. Josh hid in a bush close to the farmhouse door and watched as he thump, thump, thumped his walking stick against the door and waited for someone to respond.

"When the kindhearted lady opened the door, he said, in a halting, rhythmic voice, 'Something to eat, something to take along.' The woman nodded and disappeared, soon returning with more slices of bread and thick slices of meat, too.

"Josh practically drooled at the sight. He thought he was hidden, but his feet were sticking out of the bush. The woman came over and pulled him out. 'I don't know who you are, little boy,' she said kindly, 'but you sure look peaked. I'll get you something to eat, too.' A few minutes later, she brought him four thick beef sandwiches, and Josh was so overjoyed that he could have sung a ditty, too, like Simon's family.

"He kept on following the road walker, enjoying every bite of two sandwiches. He saved the other two for later. In the early afternoon, they came to a hollow with a small, three-sided shanty built against the hillside. The old man started a fire, got an old kettle and spoon out of the shanty, and soon had some coffee merrily boiling.

"A few more road walkers joined them there. The others eyed Josh warily, but no one told him to leave. They even gave him some of their strong coffee to drink. After they were rested and had all hit the road again, Josh wandered aimlessly along until he came to a wide bridge crossing a creek and a wide meadow.

"Parked in the meadow were five or six covered market wagons, painted with exciting designs. The horses were unhitched and resting in the shade. A few women in gaudy, brightly colored dresses were cooking something over an open fire.

"His curiosity aroused, Josh wandered close and hid among the trees and brush to watch them. A few more women sat in a circle, weaving baskets, and a group of children played happily in the meadow nearby. After awhile the children began to play a game of hide-and-seek among the trees, and Josh was discovered.

"He found himself surrounded by a group of curious, brown-eyed, gypsy children. They took a liking to him, ran off, and one by one came back with a shiny trinket to give him. The children invited Josh to join them in their play and even gave him a few much-appreciated biscuits to eat.

"Meanwhile, Josh's uncle had been looking and asking around the country for Josh. The county sheriff suggested that he check the gypsy camp, since a lot of children were running around there. Finally the uncle found Josh and took him home."

Mrs. Goldfus jumped up from her chair. "My, I've stayed way too long. I must get going."

Later, when Dannie had crawled into bed and was thinking over Josh's adventures, a daring plan began to form in his mind. Now that Silas was gone, perhaps he would run away as Josh had done. If Josh could survive, he could, too. *Nobody really wants me either. They'll be glad when they know I'm gone.*

Dannie cried into his pillow, mourning the loss of his beloved pet. He decided to hide in the woods somewhere, as soon as the weather turned warm. He hadn't seen any gypsies, beggars, or road walkers, but he would somehow find enough to eat. He would take a fishing pole and a snare and build a fire to roast his catch over the coals.

Enough of being pushed around from place to place, where he didn't feel like he belonged! He had to admit to himself that the Petersheim family was different and that he felt at home here. But he would not stay on the same farm with Lassie any longer.

Dannie fell asleep while making plans, with tears on his cheeks.

8

The Same Andrew

SPRING with all its beauty arrived once more at Whispering Brook Farm. The grass grew green, the breezes became fragrant and balmy, and pussy willows popped into blossom. The golden forsythia blazed with glory. On the morning when Omar and Nancy were leaving to make Summerville their home, a robin sang joyously from the budding maple tree, as if bidding them a blessed farewell.

The day before, word had come from Joe and Arie of the safe arrival of baby Michael Lee at Chestnut Ridge Acres. He weighed eight pounds and one ounce, and his head was covered with red fuzz.

The family planned that Omar would eat his meals with Mary and Jacob for a week while Nancy helped

Arie and Joe with the new baby.

Mary and Jacob had seen to it that the kitchen, *Sitzschtubb* (sitting room), and three bedrooms were furnished in the house at Hemlock Hill Homestead. So there really wasn't much to do on moving day.

When they arrived by van at Joe and Arie's place, Nancy eagerly hurried to the door. She could hardly wait to see her first little nephew. Nancy was proud that she would be the first of the family to see him. The rest were not coming until next week.

Joe greeted her at the door, holding the precious bundle. Nancy couldn't help gasping. "Little Michael really does have red hair!" she exclaimed.

"There's no one else in our family with red hair, is there?" She eagerly took the baby from Joe and seated herself on the settee. "A dimple in his chin, and big, wandering blue eyes," she noted. "That's typical of our family, isn't it?"

Joe answered her first question. "Arie says that she had a great-great-grandfather with a full, red beard. She also has a cousin with very red hair."

Arie came out from the bedroom, wearing a bathrobe and slippers. "I'm so glad you're here." She welcomed Nancy warmly. "Yes, it's true, my great-great-grandfather had red hair, and his name was Michael, too. Let's hope that baby Michael is as mild-mannered as he was, too."

"Oh, I'm sure he will be," Nancy declared. "My, such a sweet baby. And the house is spotless. What will I have to do besides making the meals and rocking the baby?"

"Not much," Arie admitted. "My housecleaning is all finished. But there's plenty to do in the barn."

Nancy enjoyed her week at Joe's immensely. Caring for little Michael was the best part, though she was a little anxious the first time she bathed him.

She remembered that she had read in *Die Botschaft* (a newspaper) that a girl her age had accidentally put some salt in the baby's bottle instead of sugar. But Arie assured her that nowadays doctors didn't even recommend giving extra water to a nursing baby.

Nancy had also heard of a baby being given oil of peppermint by mistake and having to be rushed to the emergency room of the hospital. In spite of her fears, the week passed pleasantly and without incident.

On the next Tuesday morning, Joe hitched Chief to the buggy for Nancy to drive over to her new home at Hemlock Hill Homestead.

"Chief has been working pretty hard these days, helping to plow," Joe told her, "so he should be nice and tame. I'm planning to go to a livestock auction on Thursday, twenty miles away. On the way home, I'll have my van driver drop me off at Omar's place, and then I'll drive Chief home."

Nancy nodded. "At least he's used to the narrow bridge at the end of the lane. I wouldn't like to have to get out and lead him or blindfold him with a shawl like you did at first. I don't foresee having any trouble with him."

She hugged baby Michael and once more kissed him on top of his fuzzy red head. Then she bade Arie and Joe good-bye, too. As she loosened Chief's tie rope, she thought bravely, *Now to be mistress of the Hemlock Hill Homestead!*

Chief trotted leisurely along, letting Nancy enjoy the scenery of freshly plowed fields. Gulls were circling overhead and alighting in the furrows to find grubs and worms. She saw red-winged blackbirds on swaying weeds along the roadside, uttering their cheery "kong-a-ree!" Wild jonquils were in bloom, nodding their merry yellow heads in the breeze.

A mile from Hemlock Hill Homestead, she spied a familiar-looking figure walking up ahead. As she came closer, she saw it was none other than Andrew Fisher. She came up beside him and reined in Chief.

"Want a ride, Andrew?" she asked. It would never do to drive by without offering it.

"Sure do." Andrew gladly hopped up on the left side of the buggy. "I'm sure glad you came along, Nancy. I walked all the way from town, and I was planning to help Omar make horse stalls today anyway. Now with you coming, I'm sure he's more than ready to have a good cook on the premises. I know you won't be burying any more *Gnepplies* (dumplings)."

Nancy blushed. So Andrew still liked to tease a bit. "Sometimes I still do make flops, though," she admitted. Then she tried to change the subject. "I hope Omar gets a dog for us."

"You won't need a dog to eat what you throw out. If you do make something Omar won't eat, you can just invite me over," Andrew offered. "I'm used to

Sally's cooking, no matter how it turns out."

"If you're ready to eat anything I cook, I just might let you," Nancy teased back. "It would probably be the first meal you ever ate in that house."

Andrew nodded. "Magees sure weren't very sociable. They were brother and sister, not husband and wife. The two were born in that house and lived together there all their lives, never marrying. I've heard that when they were children, they were playing on the ice on the big pond. The sister broke through the ice and nearly drowned. She was an invalid for the rest of her life, and he took care of her after their parents died.

"I think he was a good sort of guy, and I can't blame him for not letting us skate there. It's a spring-fed pond and has a few places were the ice doesn't freeze solid because of the springs."

Nancy agreed. "Yes, I'm sure he didn't want anyone else to suffer like his sister." After a moment of silence, she started talking about Omar's farm. "Andrew, have you ever been back in the pine bushland, up on Hemlock Hill, as we're calling it?"

"A few times," Andrew nodded. "There's a quaint little cabin back there and more than one natural spring bubbling out of the ground. It's beautiful. Hemlock Springs would be a nice name for it, too.

"Way back on the other side of the woods, there's a set of buildings where Ivor and Helga live and farm. Their last name sounds *fremm* (strange), and I can't remember it.

"They have a pet wolf—a real full-blooded wolf—

and an array of other pets such as an owl and a woodchuck. Deer are plentiful back there, too, and maybe even a bear or two, now and then. Ivor's lane is out to the other road, two miles from here."

"I can hardly wait to see it," Nancy said eagerly. "Tell Sally that I hope it suits her to go exploring with me back there sometime."

"I will," Andrew replied. "She's planning to come over with me on Friday when I return to help Omar work on his corncrib. She wants to help you get your house in shape, if you're ready to settle in."

"Fine!" Nancy said happily. "Be sure to tell her that you both are invited to stay for dinner. We're so glad for the help of good neighbors. Now that I know you won't mind eating burned *Gnepplies* and the likes, you're welcome anytime."

"We'll be there," Andrew promised. "I'll tell Sally to bring a covered dish, just in case that's all that's edible."

Nancy smiled to herself. *He's still the same Andrew, all right,* she thought. *But I'd rather have him that way than stuffy and too polite. I'm sure that underneath he has a heart of gold.*

9

How Long?

BACK at Whispering Brook Farm, Dannie was becoming more withdrawn and making more trouble. One day his foster mom noticed that her egg supply was dwindling. She decided to find out why.

Mom watched from behind a bush and made a discovery. After Dannie was finished gathering the eggs, he was making a sport of throwing some of them against the backside of the chicken house, just to be ornery. He was practicing his aim, trying to hit cracks between siding boards.

Dannie also tormented Lassie in any way he could think of. Dad had brought him an eight-week-old purebred Dalmatian pup for his very own. At first he ignored it completely, then treated it with disdain.

Finally the pup seemed to anger Dannie so much that Dad finally gave up and returned it to the former owner.

Next they bought Dannie a well-trained pony, but he took no interest in it at all. Mom and Dad were at their wits' end.

One morning Dannie stole out of bed before anyone else was up. In the predawn light, he sneaked out to the barn and opened the gate to the steer pen. Then he raced back to the house and crawled into bed again. Soon the steers were all outside, and their excited lowing woke up Lassie, who raised the alarm by ferocious barking.

Dannie came down the stairs, carrying his shoes and looking just as innocent as the other boys. The steers, with raised tails, took off for the hills, in spite of Lassie's frantic efforts to round them up.

"*Mach schnell* (quick), boys, saddle up the horses and go after them," Dad instructed. "Once they spread out all over the neighboring fields, they'll be much harder to round up."

Steven and Henry rushed to saddle two of the driving horses. Dannie, in high excitement, led his pony Dandy out of his stall, jumped on his bare back, and joined the chase. "Hi ho, Silver!" he yelled, and slapped the pony on his rump.

Mom, watching from the kitchen window, shook her head in disbelief. "See, he *has* ridden before," she noted. "Why, then, did he refuse to ride when we bought him that pony? It's hard to figure him out." She went back to frying mush and bacon for breakfast.

An hour later, the boys came straggling back for breakfast. They had managed to round up all but the ten wildest steers.

"We brought back all but ten in spite of Dannie's help," Steven said, snorting with disgust. "On his pony, he was always zigging when he should have been zagging. Sometimes it seemed like he purposely hindered rather than helped. If not, he must be mighty dumb. Ei yi yi!"

"Shh! Here he comes now," Mom said. "When he's in school, you can go after the rest."

After breakfast, Steven and Henry saddled fresh horses. With a few neighbor boys, they set out to try their hand at cowboy work. In a ravine at the back of the farm, they found the ten steers grazing contentedly. They warily raised their heads to watch the riders approaching.

"It would have been a simple thing to round up these fat spring steers if it hadn't been for Dannie," Henry pouted. "I wouldn't be a bit surprised if he was the one who left the gate open, and on purpose, too."

"Well, we have no proof," Steven replied. "But sometimes I think that a real good thrashing would do him a lot of good. He's had it coming to him for some time now. If I'd be Daed—"

"Watch out," yelled one of the other boys. "That steer's coming for you!"

It was indeed. With lowered head and a menacing bellow, it charged straight toward Steven's horse, trying to throw him to the ground. The horse stopped and braced himself. With a thud that rocked the horse and nearly sent Steven flying, the steer ran into the horse's chest. The impact staggered the steer, rolling him over in the dirt. Then, much subdued, he quietly followed the other steers to the barn.

"Whew!" Steven said shakily. "It's a good thing I wasn't riding Dandy. I wouldn't have wanted that steer to be one bit heavier. He'd probably have gored me then yet."

Back in the barn, the boys told Dad what had happened. "I'm just sure Dannie was the one who opened that gate," Henry complained. "Why don't you teach him a good lesson once? He deserves it for all his other ornery ways, too. If we'd have acted that way, I know you would not have spared the rod. We felt it many a time for less than he does."

Dad nodded. "Yes, if he'd have been properly brought up and disciplined from childhood, he wouldn't have such a struggle now to accept his lot in life. He has been deeply wounded and betrayed. For healing to take place, he has to learn to trust people again, to love and forgive others. It could be a slow process. We must be careful not to make him even more rebellious and sullen."

"How long is it going to take?" Steven complained. "I don't see any change coming."

"Dannie has always thought a lot of Omar. I have a notion that once school lets out, I'll send him out there for awhile. Omar could use a helper on the farm this summer. I'm going to have his pony trucked out, since Nancy wants him to drive while she's there."

"That's a good plan, Daed," said Henry. "Dannie

needs a fresh start so he can grow up and take responsibility."

Dad hopefully added, "Maybe on Omar's farm, Dannie will forget how he has refused to become attached to another pet. He needs to learn that to have loved and lost is better than not to have loved at all."

"Working with Omar might be good for him," Steven agreed. "He's just making a *Nixnutz* (a good-for-nothing fellow) of himself here."

"We must keep on praying for the boy and doing the best we can," Dad said. "Kindness goes a long way in such a case. We may have to return good for evil a few times yet before it gets better."

10

The Cabin

SCHOOL was over. On the first day of Dannie's summer vacation, he went with the Petersheim family out to Hemlock Hill Homestead. He had his clothes packed in a suitcase, ready to stay for several weeks or more. Dannie was looking forward to being with Omar again, his favorite "brother."

Some of Dannie's old resentments seemed to be falling off his shoulders as they got closer to Summerville. At least he would not have Lassie around to irritate him all the time! But in the back of his mind was still the idea of running away sometime, somehow, as Josh had. Then he could fend for himself, free from others bossing him around. *I'll prove I can take care of myself!* he resolved.

Nancy and Omar had found themselves quite busy on the farm. Not till Dannie arrived did they begin to think of taking time off to explore the hemlock woods and hills. Finally, one Saturday they spent the afternoon in the woods with Sally and Andrew. Dannie eagerly led the way.

At the entrance to the hemlock woods, Nancy stopped and took a deep breath. The others were also sniffing with delight. The air was spiced with the scent of sun-drenched hemlocks and firs and ferny underbrush, dappled with sunshine and shadow.

A chipmunk darted out from under a mossy log, nearly running over Dannie's foot. As he watched the chipmunk, a rabbit bounded from a thicket and hopped off into the woods.

The boy was delighted at the sights and sounds of nature. "Wow, look at that bunny run!"

"Dannie, don't you think there might be a bear or a wildcat lurking beside a tree somewhere?" Andrew asked, pretending to be worried. "Better watch out!"

"Listen!" Sally held up a hand for silence. The liquid, fluted notes of a songbird drifted down from the treetops. "Cherrie! Cherrie!" The bird alighted on a branch nearby, and there was a flash of blue wings and a rust-colored breast. "A bluebird," Sally exclaimed. "It's the first one I've seen in this neighborhood."

"I didn't realize these trees are so big," Omar remarked, glancing up at the enormous pines overhead. The wind sighed and whispered through the sweeping branches above and through the dense undergrowth, shaded with low-hanging hemlock fronds all around them.

The group heard the trickle of water around a bend and then came to the first spring, surrounded by a ring of rocks. It was clear, fresh water bubbling out of the ground and flowing into a pool. The water was so clear that they could see a school of minnows darting and swimming at the bottom.

"Oh!" Nancy exclaimed in delight. She went to her knees beside the spring, to catch some of the sparkling, crystal-clear water in her hands.

"Go ahead, taste it," Andrew told her. "It's as pure and fresh and cold as can be. But wait! Here is a bed of mint that somebody must've planted long ago. I've heard say that if you chew on a few mint leaves before you drink spring water, it makes it taste all the sweeter and colder."

Each of them took a taste of mint, then drank spring water. They all agreed that it did indeed make a difference.

Strolling on up the ferny, sun-dappled trail, they suddenly came upon a small weather-beaten cabin. It was in a clearing, surrounded by shadowy woods.

"A cabin! How enchanting!" Sally exclaimed. "Tucked in here under the trees, it almost looks like it grew here, too, like a forest toadstool. Does it really belong to your Hemlock Hill Homestead?"

"Sure does," Andrew assured her, answering for Omar. "Ivor's land doesn't start for another quarter mile. Let's take a look inside the cabin."

Dannie went first, pushing the door open, then

jumped back with a yell. "Mice!" he hollered.

"Probably squirrels, too," Omar guessed. "It's a real hideout and shelter for them."

Nancy peered into the simple small, one-room cabin, then stepped gingerly inside. "It even smells of mice in here," she said, wrinkling her nose. The floor was littered with piles of acorns, hickory nuts, shellbarks, and pinecones.

The rough-hewn stone fireplace took up most of one wall. It was littered with brown, dried-up leaves, charred old wood, and ashes from old fires.

"Say, Nancy," Sally exclaimed enthusiastically, "let's come back here sometime and give this place a good thorough cleaning. Then we can camp out here for a night or two. I've always wanted to go camping."

"Hmph!" Andrew snorted. "Wouldn't that be something! Two frightened girls in the middle of this scary wilderness. What would you do if a bear stuck its head in the door?"

"Huh! I'd be along, too, and I'd scare the bears away." Dannie was quite excited about the prospect of camping out. "I'd catch plenty of fish for us all to eat, and we could cook our meals here in the fireplace."

"You have it all figured out, Dannie," Nancy said with appreciation. "With you along, we wouldn't need to worry about a thing."

"There goes a mouse!" Sally cried. "A cute little thing, too. Must be a wood mouse."

"Let's explore some more." Nancy stepped out into the clearing again and looked around. "I wonder what exciting thing we'll see around the next bend."

"Listen!" Omar held up a hand, motioning for them to be quiet. "I hear something howling."

A second later they heard it again. "Awa–oooh-oooh-awa-ooooo!" It was a drawn-out eerie wail that sent shivers down their spines.

"What is it?" Sally whispered. "It sounds like a forlorn wild creature. Could it be a lonely coyote?"

"No, it's a wolf," Andrew said, watching Dannie's eyes grow big. "I've never heard the wolf howl before, but I'm sure it's Ivor and Helga's tame wolf. Their homestead is just around that next bend you were wondering about, Nancy. We must pay them a visit yet before we go back. They're a friendly, interesting old couple."

"But what about the wolf?" Dannie protested. "Won't he attack us?"

Andrew shook his head. "No need to fear. Ivor usually keeps the wolf chained unless he is with his master, and that's just to keep him from scaring people. Sometimes they hike through the woods together.

"Once Ivor told me that there's nothing to fear from that wolf. Under no circumstances would his pet attack a human being, as long as the wolf is not being mistreated. And I think Ivor knows as much about wild creatures as anybody. He's a genuine outdoorsman. So let's go."

11

Plenty of Pets

IT seemed like a long but enjoyable walk under the spicy, fragrant pine branches. When they reached the old couple's clearing, Ivor and Helga were sitting on the front porch of the rambling bungalow. The huge wolf was resting his head on Ivor's knee and gazing adoringly at his master.

At the sound of their footsteps, the wolf tensed and gave a low warning growl. Feeling Ivor's reassuring hand on his back, he relaxed and sank down to the porch floor.

Ivor waved his arms and called to them, "Welcome, welcome! Come on over! We're always glad to see company."

"We just heard your wolf's thrilling, spine-tingling

howl awhile ago," Andrew said, after they had all introduced themselves. "Do you think he knew we were coming?"

"Oh yes, I think so," Ivor nodded. "I can pretty well count on it. When he howls, there's something going on up there. But I assure you, there's nothing to fear."

Ivor's wife, Helga, was a plump, friendly looking woman, wearing a big ruffled apron over her plain gray dress. "Take seats," she motioned to the porch bench.

Nancy had eyes only for the wolf. He had green eyes, wide front paws, broad shoulders rippling with powerful muscles, and a glossy silvery gray fur coat. His bushy gray tail streamed regally behind him. Dannie, too, was all eyes and could not get done staring.

"A real impressive animal you have here," Omar remarked. "Where did you get him? Surely not in these woods."

Ivor smiled his friendly, crinkly-eyed smile. "No, indeed. I got him as a little bundle of fur when he was only six weeks old. He comes from Russia, my mother's homeland, where I spent a good many years long ago.

"He's the best pet we've ever had, and we've had plenty. Some of our pets have been owls, possums, chipmunks, a red fox, skunks, coyotes, and fawns. Let me show you one of the newest babies we have here."

Ivor went into the house and came back with a leaf-lined box. In it nestled a tiny baby raccoon.

"Oh!" Dannie breathed in wonderment. "What a cute little thing!" He stroked the baby's soft gray underfur with his little finger and watched it squirm and nuzzle like a newborn kitten, searching for the mother's milk.

"He's a little orphan," Ivor said sadly. "His mother was killed by a falling log when I was felling a dead tree for firewood. There were four little ones, but this is the only kit that survived. He's a sturdy, plucky little fellow."

Dannie was entranced by the little fellow, a tiny mite of fur. "How do you feed him? You'd have to use an awfully tiny bottle."

Helga chuckled. "It's a time-consuming job, day and night. We warm some milk and feed him with a straw. Would you like to take him home with you? I'd be happy to let you have him. Wouldn't you, too, Ivor?"

"He's yours, if you want him," Ivor agreed, "that is, if you're willing to give him the care he needs. Ma and I aren't used to waking up for night feedings anyhow."

"Oh, thank you, thank you!" Dannie was completely overjoyed. He had a tender heart for small, helpless animals.

"Ivor," Andrew said, "I think our new neighbors would like to hear one of your exciting animal stories." Ivor sank back into his hickory rocker, ready for his favorite hobby. He was a born storyteller and was glad he had an audience.

"Yes, sir," he began, "I've done a lot of hunting and

trapping in my time, and I suspect I know as much as anybody about it. But it's a thing of the past. No more hunting for me, especially not for sport. Now, if it would be in self-defense, that would be different.

"Let me tell you about the time I—"

Helga jumped up from her rocker. "Wait a bit, Ivor. Before you start, give me a little time to bring some refreshments for our visitors. They've had a long walk and must be hungry and thirsty."

"We'll help you," Sally offered.

Helga hurried to the kitchen, with the girls trailing her, and soon came out with a tray of some things she called kolacky. They were fancy little fruit-filled cakes and were quite delicious, too. Nancy and Sally carried out tall glasses of ice-cold mint tea for everyone.

"Did you taste the spring water on the way over?" Helga asked. "We planted a bed of mint around each spring here in the pine woods, even those over on Magee's property."

"So it was you. We must have passed about five springs on the way over, and they were all surrounded by mint. It does make the water seem even colder and fresher," Nancy told her.

Helga looked pleased. "For many years, we had no running water in the house, so those springs were important for us."

From behind the porch railing came a sound of flurried movement. Then they heard a tiny bleat, scarcely more than a whimper, and a small, trembling animal struggled up from the grass.

"Just another one of our babies," Ivor explained. "A

fawn, whose leg was injured somehow, so I brought him home to heal."

The tiny fawn, its reddish-brown coat sprinkled with silvery spots, tottered forward on unsteady legs. Its great liquid eyes blinked in the sunlight. Then it gave another pathetic little bleat as it sank to the ground again.

"Time for his bottle." Helga got up briskly. "The coon's ready to be fed, too. Come along, Dannie, and I'll show you how to feed him."

After the animal babies were fed, Ivor launched into one of his interesting stories. Nancy and Sally sank back on the bench to listen.

Dannie was all ears, and so were Omar and Andrew.

This certainly is a fascinating place, Nancy thought. Ivor and Helga were such a quaint, interesting old couple. The wolf had stretched himself out full length on the porch, his silvery gray fur gleaming in the sun.

Why, he's over six feet long, from the tip of his nose to the end of his tail, Nancy realized with a start. And, not ten feet away from the wolf's nose was the helpless, tottering little fawn.

That fawn would make a tasty meal for the wolf, according to his natural instincts! He certainly must be well trained. Then Nancy remembered a familiar chapter in the Bible. *This is like Isaiah's vision for a time when people will not hurt or destroy, and the wolf will live with the lamb. I wish we all could live like that!*

12

The Storyteller

"DID you ever hear the scream of a panther?" Ivor was asking. "No? Well, it's about the most spine-tingling, bone-chilling sound there is. Let me tell you about an adventure my great-grandfather had years ago in the mountains of Kentucky."

Ivor was making the most of entertaining his audience, keeping them spellbound and enthralled. The old man was indulging in his favorite pastime. He had such a vivid way of saying things. His listeners nearly trembled with fear and anxiety before they knew how a story would turn out.

Dannie especially was drinking in the story about hiking in the wilds and fending for oneself in pioneer days. He was gathering ideas of how to handle living by himself in the woods, with the animals. Dannie still had daydreams of striking out on his own sometime.

As the story progressed, Dannie used a twig to tickle the baby racoon in the box at his side. He thought about how much bigger a panther would be than the little coon. Both are furry animals, but one may be harmless and another may be dangerous.

All of Ivor's listeners heaved a sigh of relief at the end of the story. They felt as though they themselves had been there, watching the scenes unfold. It was truly an epic contest between man and beast.

"My great-grandpa survived his struggle with the panther, or I wouldn't be here, because my grandpa wasn't born yet," Ivor said as he finished the tale. "He skinned that panther and headed home with the hide. His wife and children were so glad to see him reach their cabin safe and sound.

"Great-grandpa tanned the panther hide and made a furry rug out of it, to put in front of his fireplace. Then he lived to tell the story to his great-grandchildren. That panther hide has been passed down to me, and I have it hanging on the wall in our living room."

"Whew!" Andrew exclaimed. "What a frightful experience!" He mopped his brow with his handkerchief.

Omar nodded. "It certainly was an exciting story. May we see that panther hide?"

"Why, sure," responded Helga. "Step right in the door, and you'll find it on the west wall. It is worn quite a bit, but it's precious to us because it's a family heirloom."

They all admired the hide and stroked its fur lightly. Then Omar said, "The shadows are getting longer, and I believe we must head for home now or we'll be late for chores. Thanks so much for letting us visit you, Helga and Ivor. I'm glad we have such good neighbors."

"That's for sure," added Nancy. "We must get together some more. Come over and visit us any time. Helga, thanks for the cookies and tea. That was just what we needed."

"Good-bye," called Sally as they left the porch.

"Dannie, come along and don't forget your little coon," Andrew said.

There was no danger of that. Dannie was still holding his new pet. Now he put the tiny animal in the box to carry home and thanked Ivor again for letting him have the baby racoon.

"Come again soon," Ivor and Helga said in unison. Ivor added, "We'll be over to see you sometime, too. After all, we have more stories to tell!"

When the hiking group had rounded a bend in the trail, the wild, eerie wail of "Awa–ooooh–oooh–awa–oooo" again echoed through the pines. Nancy shivered by reflex.

Andrew noticed and said, "Can't you just hear the cry of his ancestors in that sound? If you listen closely, you hear about years of battling for survival, fighting starvation, predators, and disease. There must be many untold stories."

Omar nodded. "You can imagine almost anything when you hear that howl. It's good that Dannie is so absorbed with his new pet. I wonder how much he was listening to that scary story. We don't want him to be getting nightmares."

Nancy was thinking, *Now if only nothing happens to that little coon like it did to the crow. A treasured pet is just what Dannie needs.*

13

Bandit

THE little raccoon spent its first few weeks with Dannie, sleeping most of the time in its soft nest of leaves. Finally he woke up to the outside world. Dannie had so faithfully cared for the helpless little fellow that he was growing bigger and rounder every day.

Dannie named him Bandit. With his black mask and sharp, beady eyes, the coon did look like a bandit. Compared to the rest of his body, Bandit's tail was long, with striking ringed sections.

One June morning Nancy awoke to the joyous chorus of singing robins, song sparrows, cardinals, and thrushes. She quickly dressed and went to the window, to breathe in great draughts of the fresh morning air and check the weather.

At the back of the yard was a thicket of wild roses, a real haven for songbirds. The fragrance of the pink-and-white blossoms lent a heady sweetness to the brisk morning air.

"It looks to be a fine day," she told herself happily, stretching her arms high. Then, through the curtain at the side of the window, a movement on the balcony caught her attention, so she drew back.

There stood Dannie by the railing, with Bandit on his arm. He was surveying the fine morning and Hemlock Hill Homestead, just as she loved to do each day. But there was a sad look on his face, and he reached up and brushed a tear from his cheek.

Why, he's crying, Nancy realized. *The poor boy! I'm sure he's lonesome for his dad, and probably for his mother, too. He seems to like it here. But I sure don't blame him for missing his parents, and he never even had any brothers and sisters.*

Nancy resolved to be extra nice to Dannie, no matter what he did. He had been so taken up with caring for his new pet these past weeks that he had no thoughts of getting into mischief. But now she knew that he still had moments of feeling deep pain and loneliness.

Curious, Nancy watched the boy and his pet. Bandit seemed to sense his master's mood in an uncanny way. He reached up with a humanlike paw and patted Dannie's arm, chirring in his soft, insistent way Was he trying to comfort the boy?

A smile spread over Dannie's face, and he turned

and went back into his room with Bandit.

Why, they seem to understand each other! Nancy marveled. *That must be a real consolation to Dannie to have a loyal friend like that. Now I'm sure he's not a bad boy at all—just hurt and confused.*

Pinning on her apron, she went down to the kitchen. "Mmm, fresh strawberries for breakfast," Nancy told Omar when he came in from choring. "Mary sent some over with Jacob yesterday."

She set the bowl of sliced strawberries on the table. Dannie, with Bandit still on his arm, came over to the table. Spying the berries, Bandit leaped onto the table. With his adept little "hands," he reached into the bowl and helped himself to a strawberry half.

Chattering and chirring with anticipation, Bandit went to the water glass set at Omar's plate and swished the berry round and round in the water. Then he bit off a dainty piece, tilted his head back, and chewed happily, with a satisfied look on his face. This all was such a comical performance that the watchers could not help but laugh.

The little coon seemed to sense that he had an audience and could show off. With an eager look on his mobile face, he reached over to the plate of bread and pulled a slice toward him. His tiny, humanlike hands pinched off a small piece and rolled it into a ball. Before anyone could stop him, Bandit started to dunk the bread ball into a cup of hot chocolate at Dannie's place.

The chocolate wasn't steaming hot but was warm enough that Bandit gave a cry of startled dismay. He drew back and ran to the safe shelter of Dannie's arms. Bandit whimpered sadly and tried to nuzzle into his shirtsleeve.

Omar clucked his tongue in sympathy and said kindly, "It's a hard world out there, isn't it, little coon?" He noticed that Dannie looked sad. "I guess we all have to learn to take the bad with the good, sometime or other. Going through the school of hard knocks isn't easy."

Turning to Nancy, Omar said, "Andrew was over this morning on the scooter. He asked me to go with him to the livestock auction today. Sally wants you to come along and be dropped off at Fisher's place to help her with their oodles of strawberries, if it suits you. Dannie, do you want to go along to the livestock auction?"

"Sure do!" Dannie was all eagerness, with no trace of tears now. "And I'll take Bandit with me, too!"

In the days that followed, Dannie hardly ever let Bandit out of his sight. He was more fiercely protective of his little pet than ever. Dannie carried him around on his shoulder most all the time, even while working.

On the upstairs balcony, Nancy had fixed a soft bed in a chicken crate for Bandit. But one midnight, Omar heard a chirring sound. He lit a kerosene lamp and went into Dannie's room. There on the pillow beside the sleeping Dannie, Bandit lay curled up peacefully, his little hands on top of the blanket.

Bandit opened his eyes, looking half pleadingly up at Omar, with his bright little goggle eyes. His small button nose was twitching slightly.

Omar went back to his bed, shaking his head in disbelief. *Oh, well,* he thought, *Bandit seems perfectly housebroken and clean, so I guess it's really no worse than a pup.*

14

Cherry Cobbler

NANCY and Sally worked together doing strawberries. A bit later, the cherries ripened, providing more opportunities to work together.

There was a huge old black cherry tree in the meadow below the hemlock woods. Omar, Andrew, and Dannie brought in bucket after bucket of the small delicious black cherries. They reported that Dannie ate almost as much as he put into the pail. But Bandit was even worse. He ate every one he picked.

Nancy and Sally pitted and canned the cherries almost as fast as their brothers could pick them. In the midst of this cherry-flurry, with cherry-juice stains all over the kitchen counter, and table, they heard a knock on the back door, by the washstand.

Nancy peeked out through the houseplants on the windowsill. "Why, it's Helga!" she gasped in surprise, hurrying to open the door. "Do come in!" she invited the friendly, smiling old lady. "We're in the middle of doing cherries, so you must excuse our mess."

"I came to help," Helga told them. "It doesn't take many cherries for Ivor and me anymore, but I do like to make a few good pies and cobblers every year. Ivor had walked back to the hemlock springs, as we call them, and saw Omar and Andrew up in the tree. That's what brought us over."

"Where's the wolf?" Sally wondered. "Did he come along?"

"Oh no, he's at home, securely chained," Helga replied. "He's not really temperamental, but we never take him visiting. Someone might be frightened and have a heart attack.

"And how is the little raccoon doing? We were wondering so much, we thought we just had to come and see."

"Splendid!" Nancy could truthfully say. "He sure means a lot to Dannie." Nancy handed Helga a bowl of cherries to pit. "If you really meant that you want to help, maybe I'll let you make a cobbler. Then I'll invite you all to stay for supper and help to eat it. I've heard say that you are a very good cook."

"It's a bargain." Helga beamed at the praise. "I don't mean to brag, but Ivor says my cobblers are hard to beat."

At that moment Ivor opened the back screen door

brought in yet another pail of the little black cherries. "We certainly came on the right day," he bantered. "It's a lucky thing that I walked back to the springs, for it sure looks like you all could use some help."

"At least we succeeded in getting ourselves invited for supper," Helga told him. "I'm going to make a cherry cobbler."

"Lucky day!" Ivor responded. He hurried back outside with his empty bucket, a big smile on his face.

With Helga's capable and experienced hands helping, the work seemed to fly. Her interesting stories made the task of seeding the small cherries seem less tedious. She proved herself to be a superb storyteller, every bit as good as Ivor.

"When I was a little girl," she began, "we lived on the edge of a wilderness where bears and other varmints still roamed. One day my mother sent my little sister and me out into the woods to pick huckleberries. "We found the berry patch torn up, and a big mother brown bear with two little cubs was hanging around. She came after us, and we ran. . . ."

Sally and Nancy were becoming so absorbed in Helga's story that they slowed their cherry pitting. But Helga's hands kept pace with her lips. Now she was working the dough with her hands and getting ready to bake the cobbler. With her years of experience, she did not need a cookbook.

Helga deftly rolled the cobbler dough and transferred it to the pan. "We got lost and asked the good Lord to take care of us and help us find our way home."

She paused, as if remembering every detail of that long-ago escapade. Then she went on with the tale, keeping the girls entertained as they worked and the cobbler baked. Finally the story was finished, and so was the cobbler.

"I suppose guardian angels were watching over us, protecting us from the wild animals. We walked many miles, but in the wrong direction. Our parents hunted all night through the wilderness, calling for us until they found us."

"All's well that ends well," Nancy said with a sigh of relief. "I'm glad there are no panthers or wolverines or grizzly bears here in the hemlock woods."

"There may be a few black bears around occasionally," Helga told her. "But there's nothing to fear, unless you corner them or bother their cubs. Otherwise, they are more afraid of you than you would be of them. There are plenty of deer, though, and they seem to be increasing."

Helga's cobbler turned out to be scrumptious, dripping with sweet cherry juice. When Jacob stopped in with a big dish of homemade vanilla ice cream, it made a perfect combination for dessert. That topped off the supper's main course, Nancy's casserole with beef, potatoes, and vegetables.

Ivor showed his satisfaction: "This was a jolly good meal, fit for any regal little coon."

Bandit was at his usual place at the table, seated on an old wooden tray. Dannie had taught him to stay there and was tossing Bandit enough tidbits to keep him happy.

"You'd better be sure to keep an eye on your pet when that patch of early sweet corn is ready," Ivor warned. "Better start building a cage now."

Dannie just mumbled, "We'll see."

When the old couple was ready to leave, Ivor brought it up again. "Trying to keep a smart little raccoon away from a sweet corn patch is like trying to keep a bee away from blossoms."

He winked and smiled at Dannie. But Nancy saw a fleeting look of defiance flash into Dannie's eyes, as if he were thinking, *Bandit can have all the sweet corn he wants and whenever he wants it.*

Nancy didn't say anything, but she thought, *We'll see about that. I'm sure Dannie has no idea how much damage a little coon can quickly do in a corn patch.*

15

Cat and Coon

ON Monday morning, Nancy awoke to hear the music of raindrops on the back balcony roof. She snuggled back under the sheets contentedly, thinking, *The cherries are all canned, the sweet corn's not ready yet, and I can't work outside in the rain. So there won't be much to do today. Hmm! I wish I'd have a good book to read.*

A moment later, Nancy jumped out of bed in the blink of an eye, her heart pounding with fear. The air was rent with shrill cries of furious pain and wild catlike yells that sounded much like a panther's wild scream, Nancy imagined.

"*Was in die Welt* (what in the world)?" Nancy exclaimed. She pulled on her dress with shaky hands and dashed down the stairs. On the back stoop, she was horrified to see an awful tangle of yellow cat fur and gray-and-black coon fur. Cat and coon were struggling and wrestling, spitting and hissing.

Dannie was trying to pull them apart, getting himself scratched and nipped in the process. Nancy had a sudden inspiration. Inside the washhouse door was a bucket of cold water. She quickly grabbed it and dumped all of it on top of the squirming mass of fury.

With a sputtering and shaking of heads, the two culprits backed off. Dannie gave the big yellow tomcat a well-aimed kick that sent him fleeing for cover in the wild rose thicket. Then he gingerly picked up the battered little Bandit, who was chirring and trilling sadly, though not seriously hurt. Bandit was trying to examine his wounds with his humanlike little hands.

"Dirty old tomcat!" Dannie muttered, carrying the little raccoon into the kitchen. "Get me the iodine, Nancy, and some bandages."

Omar, coming in for breakfast, had missed the whole thing, except for seeing the tomcat streak for cover in the thicket. He shook his head sadly. "That's something I hadn't thought of. Maybe it's even against the law to have a pet raccoon because it might spread rabies. It's law that we have to have our dogs and cats vaccinated. But that stray tom, how are we supposed to know?"

Dannie's eyes widened with fear. "I don't care what you say!" he cried, stamping his foot. "No one's taking Bandit from me!" He clutched his pet and ran upstairs to his room, banging the door behind him.

"Oh, dear, what will become of Dannie yet?" Nancy sighed. "Couldn't we just have the vet give the little coon his rabies shots?"

"Probably," Omar agreed. "The vet's coming out in a few days anyway, and I'll ask him about it. Meanwhile, I'll try to catch the tomcat in a trap and hold it to watch for signs of rabies."

A short time later, Nancy was clearing the breakfast table. Glancing out the kitchen window, she saw Fisher's plucky pony coming in the lane. Sally was sitting in the pony cart, sheltered by an umbrella.

"Hurrah, Omar, look who's coming!" Nancy cried delightedly. "Good old Sally! If anybody can liven up a rainy day, she's the one. I wonder what brings her over here through the drizzle."

Omar went out to help Sally unhitch. "Hello," she greeted him merrily. "I'm staying all day, if it suits. Is Nancy going to be home?"

"Sure is!" Omar smiled. "You should have heard her cheer when she saw you drive in. Let me put the pony in the barn for you."

Sally dashed to the house, where Nancy met her at the door. "I have material to make a new dress," Sally explained, "and Mom said I may make it here, if you don't mind. You could help with the handwork." She held up the dress goods, made of soft, shimmering lavender.

"It's beautiful!" Nancy cried. "I think I'll get myself one like it, too." The girls worked together all forenoon, chattering happily away. By the time Omar came in for dinner, Sally was trying on the dress to make sure it would fit. Nancy was pinning up the hem and making it even all around.

"Whoo–eeee!" Omar's whistle even brought Dannie down from his room in a hurry, carrying Bandit on his pillow. "See the lovely lady!" Omar said to Dannie. "Doesn't she look like a queen?"

Dannie was in a sour mood and quickly retorted, "She looks like an old hen, sprouting and puffing her feathers!"

Sally was helping Nancy pin the hem and had a pin between her teeth. She burst out laughing, then suddenly gulped and covered her mouth with her hand, a look of horror on her face. "The pin!" she gasped. "I—I've swallowed a pin! *Was muss ich duh* (what shall I do)?"

The others stared at her in dismay. Sally moaned, "I just—I just read last week in *Die Botschaft* (newspaper) that a woman in Canada swallowed a pin and died from it."

"Oh, that happened years ago," Nancy said, trying to comfort her.

Sally was fast turning as white as a sheet. In a moment she crumpled into a heap on the floor, in her new lavender dress.

"Quick, Omar, she's fainted." Nancy was near tears. "We can't just let her lie there. Carry her to the settee, and I'll get water to sprinkle on her face."

Omar put Sally on the settee, and a few seconds later, she was sitting up, with color returning to her face.

"*Elend* (misery)!" she muttered as she sipped some

water. "This never happened to me before."

"Ya well, you never swallowed a pin before, did you?" Nancy asked. "Do you feel all right?"

Sally nodded weakly. "When I felt that pin sliding down my throat, I just simply panicked. But say, Nancy, weren't we using safety pins?"

Nancy nodded, light dawning in her eyes. "Maybe it isn't so bad after all."

"The one I had was still closed, because I was just handing you the pins, and you opened them as you used them.

So it shouldn't harm me. How silly it was of me to panic like that."

Nevertheless, Sally seemed much subdued. She left for home without even staying for dinner, as she had planned to do.

After she left, Nancy scolded her brother. "Omar Petersheim, I'm surprised at you for whistling at Sally like that and saying what you did. That's probably what flustered her so much that she swallowed the pin, not what Dannie said."

Omar's face reddened. "I really don't know what ailed me. I was ashamed of myself as soon as I had done it. What will Sally think of me now?"

Changing the subject, he turned to Dannie. "Let me see your little coon. How deep are his scratches?"

After examining Bandit, Omar said, "Hmm, they don't look too bad. I think they'll heal pretty fast.

"I caught that old tomcat in a trap this afternoon. I found a half-eaten chicken on the barn bank, maybe left by a skunk. That's what lured the cat out of the thicket. Now we'll keep him penned up for a few weeks and see if he has rabies."

So Dannie was comforted that evening. But down deep in his heart, he was afraid that he might lose his beloved pet. That deepened his resolve to run away, somehow, sometime. *All I have to do is work out the plans*, he thought. *I'm not taking any chances on losing Bandit.*

16

Threshing Time

AT Omar's farm, it was time to harvest the wheat. Omar had borrowed one of Jacob's horses so he would have three workhorses to pull the heavy binder. The binder cut the wheat and used twine to tie it into sheaves. Nancy came out and helped Omar and Dannie set the sheaves up into shocks to dry for a week or so.

In all the excitement leading up to threshing day, Dannie forgot his ideas of running away. Early in morning, the owner of the threshing machine came in the lane with his outfit. He put it in position, and Jacob strung the big drive belt from the John Deere engine to the threshing machine.

A crew of eight men with extra teams and wagons

arrived to help. After the dew was off the shocks, the first wagonload of sheaves came in from the field. Jacob turned the big flywheel and started the engine. The threshing machine shuddered and gradually picked up speed. It groaned and worked hard when the bundles were thrown into the feeder.

The thresher chopped the sheaves open and beat the heads of wheat. Then the precious grains ran out of the hopper spout and into waiting sacks. The straw flew out of the blower and into the straw mow. It would be used to bed the animals.

Dannie's job was to watch that no wheat was spilled onto the ground. He climbed up into the box wagon where he could better keep an eye on what was happening.

Back in the house, Sally had arrived to help Nancy cook for the threshing crew. "Oh, Sally," Nancy cried in relief, "you're the most welcome sight I ever saw. I sure can use some help."

Already she was tired and flustered. There was so much to do and remember. This was Nancy's first time as head cook for a threshing gang. Later Mary would be over to help if she was feeling better by then. She had been bothered by hay fever.

"Just tell me what to do," Sally said sympathetically. "We're in this together."

"Okay, you can bring in two heads of cabbage from the garden. I just noticed that it's ready. Fresh coleslaw will be a welcome change from chowchow. Then there's a pail of potatoes in the washhouse to peel, and the meat loaf to put into casserole dishes.

Oh yes, the late peas are picked but aren't *blicked* (hulled) yet, and—"

"Whoa there!" Sally exclaimed. "One thing at a time, please. I can't think that fast."

"Sorry," Nancy said ruefully. "I guess I was just thinking aloud. Oh, yes, then we need to put tubs of water out under the shade tree by the pump, for the men to wash up. Threshing is dirty work. The bench and clean towels must be taken out. Don't let me forget anything."

The girls worked hard and managed to have the dinner ready on time, even though Mary never did show up. The long table was set, the water glasses filled with a few ice cubes in each glass, and the homemade bread was sliced and covered with tea towels.

The *gschtammde Grummbiere* (mashed potatoes) were light and fluffy after Sally and Nancy took turns mashing them for fifteen minutes. The aroma of the baked meat loaf filled the kitchen, and the gravy was free of lumps.

"Do you think the food we prepared will reach around?" Nancy asked worriedly. "There are all those hungry hardworking men. What if there's not enough?"

"Don't worry," Sally laughed gaily. "If it gets all, we'll bring some more jars out of the cellar. There's vegetable soup to heat, or canned sausage and string beans, or tomato soup, or—"

"Hush!" Nancy cried. "You're such a comfort. Here come the men. Let's dish the food out now."

For the next half hour, Nancy and Sally were kept busy filling and refilling and passing the dishes, and refilling water glasses. The hungry menfolk ate heartily.

With a sigh of relief, Nancy saw that there was plenty to reach around, with raspberry pie and ice cream for dessert. After thanking the girls for the good meal, the men filed out the door. They rested under the shade trees for a quarter hour or so before heading back to work.

"Finally we can fill our plates and eat, too," Sally said gratefully. "We'll be needing our strength to wash all those stacks of dishes."

Nancy nodded. "At least our work is not as hard as threshing. We have it easy in here compared to the men working under the hot sun. But I'm sure Dannie is enjoying himself to the fullest."

"Say, where is that little coon of his?" Sally wondered. "I haven't seen it since I'm here."

"Sleeping," Nancy replied. "He sleeps most of the day when the weather's so warm. I wouldn't be surprised if he spends his nights prowling around, spying out my sweet-corn patches. I don't know what we'll do when the corn is ripe."

Out in the field that afternoon, Dannie worked with the men for awhile, manning a hayfork to pitch the sheaves onto the wagon. Sweat poured down his forehead, and he used his handkerchief to mop his brow.

Dannie's shirt was made of a light blue, cool cotton material, but he thought it was still too warm. He opened the buttons and slipped out of it, and a cooling breeze fanned his bare skin.

That's better, he thought, tossing his shirt onto the wagon. *Working in this heat shouldn't be so bad now. No hot, sticky shirt clinging to me.*

He pitched a few more sheaves, relishing the feeling of freedom. But then he heard Omar shouting to him from the next wagon to put his shirt back on. "I might have known I'd get scolded," Dannie pouted.

He had been pitching some sheaves from beside the horses and headed for the wagon to get his shirt. Just then, the lead horse swung his head around so the blinders beside his eyes would let him see what the shouting was about.

When the lead horse saw Dannie without a shirt, his head shot up, and he snorted. The other horse eyed Dannie warily, too. What was this strange-looking shirtless apparition?

The horses had never seen such a sight before. Suddenly the team spooked and bolted. Their big hooves thundered on the ground as they galloped. They didn't slow down until they reached the barn, where Jacob caught them. Sheepishly, Dannie headed to the barn to get his shirt from the wagon.

Nancy and Sally had taken lemonade and cookies out to the threshing machine for a mid-afternoon snack for the men. They were astounded to see Dannie disappear into the barn minus his shirt.

Nancy sighed. "Dannie knows our menfolk don't walk around like that. Besides, it's a good way to get a dreadful sunburn."

"I wouldn't blame him too much," Sally observed. "Before he came to live with your family, I'm sure he was used to going without a shirt in the summertime. He was likely wearing shorts, too, like the *Englischer* (non-Amish) do."

"Yes. I guess you're right," Nancy agreed. "But sometimes I have to wonder if our teachings will ever rub off on him, though."

17

Escape

A WEEK later, after helping Omar finish the barn chores, Nancy went to the sweet corn patch to see if the corn was ripe enough to bring in their first meal. Some of the corn was ready. She happily filled her dishpan with a dozen golden, tender ears to take to the house.

Dannie was hoeing the potato rows nearby, with Bandit on his shoulder as usual. On hearing the "sherk, sherk, sherk" sound of Nancy husking the cobs, he perked up his ears. Some instinct, likely handed down from his ancestors, told him that here was something of great interest. Or maybe it was just a coon's natural curiosity.

Bandit climbed down from his perch and watched

unnoticed as Nancy pulled ear after ear from the stalks and twisted off the husks. With his dark masked eyes glittering greedily and his ringed tail twitching from side to side, he took everything in.

Finally, when Nancy had her back turned, he ran to the dishpan, stole one of the ears, and ran off with it. After the first tasty bite, Bandit was hooked. Never before had he tasted anything that pleased his palate so thoroughly. Greedily, he consumed the whole ear, then watched carefully as Nancy pulled off the last ear and stripped down the husk.

As soon as Nancy had left for the house, he scurried up the next cornstalk and pulled it gradually all the way to the ground. The rest was easy, eating the juicy, tender kernels as fast as he could tear layers of husk away. Then he tackled the next stalk, and the next, taking only a few bites from each ear.

He was on a spree of unruly sampling and exploration—living up to his name, Bandit. At first when Dannie saw what his pet was doing, he doubled over with laughter at the coon's frantic antics. But then he sobered quickly. Ivor had said he would need to build a cage. No way would Dannie pen Bandit up in a cage.

He tore the coon away from his reveling and walked off with him. It was time to make some serious plans for running away. When Nancy went to get more sweet corn for supper, she was indignant when she saw the damage that Bandit had done. She ran to the barn to find Omar, who had just come in from the field and was unhitching the big workhorses.

"That coon!" Nancy burst out. "We're have to pen him up right now! Omar, come and see the damage Bandit did in the corn patch."

Just then Nancy spied Dannie inside the barn door, listening, and she cringed at the defiant look on his face. Omar saw it, too.

"We have to do something," he agreed. "We could try a low electric fence, powered by a battery. Someone recently suggested draping dirty laundry around the cornstalks to scare off animals.

"Dannie, you'll have to be sure to lock Bandit up tonight," he instructed. "He could ruin the patch completely in one night."

"There are several more batches of corn that are just about ready too," added Nancy.

That evening at the supper table, Nancy munched on her steaming, tantalizing ear of corn and pondered the situation. She came up with what she thought might be a solution to the problem, and she sounded it out to Omar and Dannie.

"You know, Arie told me that they don't have any early sweet corn this year. Their early corn blighted, and now they won't be having any at all till the end of August and on into September. Maybe it would be a good idea for Dannie and Bandit to spend a few weeks at Joe's place till our early corn is over. Then we wouldn't have to lock Bandit up."

Omar's eyes lit up. "That just might solve the problem." He turned to Dannie, "Would you like to stay with Joe and Arie at the Chestnut Ridge farm for a few weeks? He could use a helper like you, now that

Steven is no longer working for him. You've been there before, haven't you?"

Dannie nodded and shrugged his shoulders. "Whatever. It would be better than penning up Bandit." To himself he thought, *If I don't like it there, I'll just run away.*

"I don't have time to take you over this evening," Omar said. "But the feed salesman is stopping in here tonight to drop off some samples of supplements. Then he's going to leave some at Joe's place, too. You could catch a ride with him. He's a friendly old chap."

"Lucky you," Nancy said enviously. "You'll get the chance to hold baby Michael all you want!"

"Yeah, great!" Dannie pretended to be disgusted, but Nancy sensed that underneath he did seem fairly enthusiastic about going. She had no idea of the plans brewing in his mind.

Dannie eagerly packed some clothes in his satchel, got his fishing line and hooks, a flashlight, his slingshot, and the Barlow pocketknife that Andrew had given him. Secretly he stashed a few packets of book matches in his shirt pocket.

Nancy pulled off a dozen ears of corn to share with Joe's. "This will be a complete surprise to them," Nancy told him. "They have no idea you're coming, but they will be glad to take you in. After all, Joe's our brother."

When Nancy went to the barn to finish the chores, Dannie helped himself to a packet of dried beef from the cellarway, a pack of crackers, a chunk of cheese, and some dried apples. Surely Nancy wouldn't miss that, and he felt that he had earned the supplies.

Dannie wanted to be prepared, in case he decided to head for the hills with Bandit. He still didn't feel easy about that rabies business. Besides, camping out in the summertime would be fun.

The feed salesman readily agreed to take Dannie along over to Joe's in his rattling old truck. "I may make you walk in the lane, over that narrow bridge, though, at Joe's place," he told the boy. "I've gone over the bridge, and my truck is not too wide for it. But since I'm in a hurry tonight—You don't have too much to carry in, do you?"

"Nope," Dannie told him. "I'll be glad to walk in."

He was thinking, *It's a good thing he doesn't know why.* A daring plan was taking shape in Dannie's thoughts. Things just might work out well for him after all.

"That's a good little coon you have there," the salesman said, eyeing Bandit. "Bet he doesn't ever get into any mischief."

"Nope," Dannie said again, trying not to think of the damaged sweet corn.

"He just does what little coons are supposed to do, doesn't he?"

Dannie nodded. "He's my best friend."

In no time at all, it seemed, they had traveled the four miles to Joe's and were stopping at the narrow bridge. "Will you give Joe these packets of supplement samples?" the driver asked, handing Dannie a bag. "Are you sure you don't have more than you can handle?"

"Oh no," Dannie assured him. "If my load is too heavy, I can come out later with the scooter and get the sweet corn."

"Take good care of that coon." With a wave of his hand, the driver pulled away.

Dannie sat on the edge of the bridge, staring into the clear, gurgling, rushing water. Here was his chance. Joe and Arie didn't know he was coming. No one would miss him. *But what about those supplements I'm supposed to give to Joe?*

His eyes fell on Joe's mailbox, and quickly he stuffed the bag inside. Luckily, the leafy branches of the trees along the road prevented anyone at the house or barn from seeing him at this end of the bridge. Bandit was chirring excitedly, seeing minnows darting about in the water. Dannie picked him up and put him on his shoulder.

"Time to go, before someone comes along," he told Bandit. He picked up his gear and the sweet corn, heading for the deeper part of the woods, intending to backtrack until he reached the hemlock woods on Omar's place.

"That little cabin will make an excellent hideaway, and those cold springs will give me fresh, pure water," he muttered. Dusk was fast descending, and bullfrogs were croaking from the marshes. Bandit was trilling his excitement from Dannie's shoulder, sensing adventure ahead. Dannie, too, felt a twinge of excitement stirring in his veins. *This will be a real adventure,* he thought.

It was quite a challenge, being on his own like this!

He figured that if it took all night to get to the cabin, tomorrow he could sleep all day if he wished. There would be no one to tell him what to do.

"Bandit and I will be fine," Dannie bragged to himself. "I'm tired of being treated like a baby. I'll prove to everyone that I can take care of myself. I won't have to be sent from place to place and have my pets killed and mistreated."

Nevertheless, as the darkness of the woods deepened around Dannie, a wave of homesickness engulfed him. "If only my dad could be here with me," he sighed. "Then it would be perfect."

18

A Hemlock Mattress

AFTER resting awhile on a fallen log, Dannie trudged on again through the dense green woods. He kept the road in sight so he would not lose his way. From his perch on the boy's shoulder, Bandit trilled softly, entranced by the sounds around them, the calling of the night insects, the chorus of the frogs, and the rustlings of wings nearby.

Fireflies dotted the countryside, and a silvery new moon rose above the treetops. The rustlings of mice and other small creatures in the grasses made Dannie feel jumpy. Bandit's small dark eyes darted to and fro, trying to take in everything at once.

They crossed an open hay field and were startled by a weird "whooo, whooo, whooo" close by. That started chills along Dannie's spine until he realized it was only a hoot owl, hunting for mice. The skies were softly velvet and dusky, but while they crossed stretches of fragrant, growing cornfields, the night seemed black as midnight.

Finally, near a winding little stream, Dannie set down his satchel, corn, and gear. He sank tiredly to the ground. Bandit promptly climbed up on the bag and helped himself to an ear of corn. Chirring eagerly, he proceeded to tear off the husk with his little humanlike hands. He sank his teeth into the juicy kernels, feasting to his heart's content.

By now the moon was high, with clouds obscuring it some of the time. After a short rest, Dannie started off again. Seeing the lights of a village ahead in the distance, they made a wide detour, hoping that no stray dogs would come after them, bark, and call attention to them.

Much later Dannie was so tired from all he was carrying. He was tempted to stop right where he was, curl into a ball, and sleep. But something seemed to tell him that would not be wise. After another rest, he wearily trudged onward. Then, around the next bend, he spied the outline of Omar's place and Hemlock Hill just ahead in the darkness.

"Hurrah, Bandit, we made it," Dannie cried happily. "Our journey's almost over!"

Bandit trilled softly in reply.

For a moment Dannie was tempted to sneak into the house and crawl into his soft clean bed. But then the worry of losing Bandit made him head toward the woods. He gave the buildings a wide berth, skirted the pond by a hundred yards or more, and headed for the hill.

A moment later a soft splash stopped him in his tracks. Something was moving down by the pond. He strained his eyes in the darkness, trying to see what it was. "Why, it's a deer!" he whispered. A big buck!"

In the starlight he could faintly see the deer's big rack of antlers as he swam steadily across the pond. Breathlessly, Dannie watched him climb out on the other shore, then disappear into the darkness, going toward the hemlock woods. It was the first live deer that Dannie had ever seen, except at a zoo.

"Let's go, Bandit." Dannie was no longer tired. "We'll probably see a lot more of those big beauties yet before we go back to civilization."

Following the same trail they had taken the day they visited Ivor and Helga, the boy and the coon were soon deep in the dark, shadowy woods. Dannie suddenly shivered. A disturbing thought had stopped him in his tracks: *What if Ivor's big wolf is loose and roaming about in these woods?*

Hearing rustlings in the thicket, he shone his flashlight all around him nervously. Seeing nothing, he fearfully but bravely strode onward. It seemed much further to the old cabin now than it had on that pleasant afternoon walk.

Finally they came to the mint-overgrown spring, stopped for a refreshing drink, and rested. The warm night air was scented with the odor of spicy hemlock branches and ferny undergrowth.

As they hiked further, a rabbit bouncing off into the woods startled Dannie so that he stopped, ready for flight. He half expected to see a wolf or a bear coming for him. But the beam of his flashlight revealed only the cottontail bobbing away, and the pair trudged on.

At last they reached the little clearing around the cabin. Dannie stopped and set down his burdens. A wind had sprung up and was sighing and whispering through the piney branches above.

Even before Dannie pulled open the creaking door, he heard the scampering of little feet inside. Bandit chirred questioningly from his shoulder, reaching out a little hand to Dannie's cheek for reassurance.

"Just squirrels and mice," Dannie told him in a low voice. "At least I hope there are no rats and skunks."

He quickly shone his flashlight around the room and saw flurried movements in the shadowy corners for a bit. Then all was still. The floor was still littered with pinecones and old brown leaves, along with lots of hickory nutshells, acorns, and shellbarks. The air smelled musty.

Dannie went to one of the bunks built against the wall and brushed off the remains of many a squirrel's feast. "Tomorrow this place has to be thoroughly cleaned and aired," he decided. But for tonight he was only concerned about making a comfortable bed.

Taking Bandit with him, he went outside to the nearest hemlock tree. He broke down small boughs, twisted them, and struggled to cut them off with his pocketknife. When he had a pile, he carried them into the cabin and set to work, carefully arranging the boughs on the bunk.

Back outside, he cut several armloads of soft tips from more hemlock boughs. He spread them evenly over the boughs on the bunk, making a soft, spongy mattress fit for a king. Out of his satchel, he got his two pairs of spare pants and two shirts and spread them over the hemlock mattress.

"There!" he said to Bandit, with a smile of tired satisfaction. "It's a top-notch bed, soft and springy as you could wish."

Bandit trilled his agreement. Whatever his master did was fine with him.

Dannie went outside and brought in the bag of sweet corn and his fishing line. "Can't have any varmints stealing our breakfast," Dannie told Bandit. He barred the old but solid door with the rusty clasp at the side. Dannie set the bag of sweet corn up on the stone mantel above the fireplace, hoping the little creatures sharing the cabin wouldn't find it there.

Then he gratefully stretched out on the fragrant hemlock bed, with a glad feeling of accomplishment and satisfaction. *At last I've really done it, run away to be on my own.*

Bandit, curled up beside him, was soon fast asleep. But for a long time, Dannie lay awake, listening to the constant scurrying of little feet on the cabin floor. "I'm not afraid of a few mice and squirrels," he scoffed, to reassure himself. "I aim to make friends with them soon anyway."

Dannie was very tired, more tired than he had ever

been before. His muscles ached so that he was afraid he wouldn't be able to sleep at all. But his hemlock mattress was so comfortable and the odor of the spicy branches so delightful that he soon relaxed completely. He fell asleep with a smile on his face and hemlock fragrance in every breath.

The runaway boy was completely oblivious to the fact that at that very moment, just outside the cabin in the clearing, a huge wild-looking shaggy gray wolf was sniffing out his trail. The wolf even came right to the door of the cabin, then trotted off toward home.

So soundly asleep were Dannie and Bandit that neither of them heard, from the depths of the woods, the lonely and wild-sounding wail of Ivor's wolf. It echoed back from the hills: "Awa—oooooh–oooh–ooh–awa–ooooooo."

19

The Best Meal

DANNIE awoke the next morning to sunshine streaming in through the old dusty, cobwebby windowpanes of the cabin. A crinkling, rustling sound from the direction of the fireplace, made him spring off the bed in alarm. Then he burst out laughing at the comical sight.

Bandit was up on the mantel and had managed to take an ear of corn out of the bag. He was tearing off the husks and, with a look of great relish, gobbling up the juicy golden kernels.

"Little thief," Dannie said affectionately. "My stomach is growling, too, but I don't want to eat mine raw."

Boiling a few ears of corn was easier said than

done. It had just dawned on him that there was no kettle for cooking, even if he could start a fire. He waited until Bandit was through feasting, then together they went out to the spring. He chewed on some mint leaves, then drank big swallows of the cold sweet, pure water. That was quite refreshing.

Dannie noticed with delight that morning in the woods was a lot pleasanter than nighttime. The pines and hemlocks were now drenched with golden sunshine that brought out the natural fragrance all the more.

High in the trees, squirrels whisked from branch to branch, scolding and chattering at this invasion of their domain. A pert, tiny chipmunk ran by so close that he startled Bandit before disappearing under a tree root. In the clear shallow pool beside the bubbling spring, little minnows darted about, enjoying the warming sunshine.

Bandit, seeing the quick movements of the minnows, lost no time in waddling over to the pool. Chirring excitedly, he circled the pool, his dark little masked eyes following every movement. Then he waded in. Scarcely more than a minute later, he triumphantly held up a wriggling minnow in his skilled humanlike hands, for Dannie to see.

Dannie watched fascinated as Bandit swished the tiny fish back and forth in the water before he sat on the bank to eat it. He wondered why the little coon so readily ate sweet corn without washing it first.

"That takes care of your breakfast, little buddy," Dannie said out loud. "But I'm still as hungry as can be. C'mon, let's follow the trail. Maybe I can find some berries."

He swung Bandit up to his shoulder, and they started off. It was a sparkling morning. From high up in the branches of a pine tree, a bright red cardinal called, "What cheer! What cheer! What cheer!" A dew-drenched spiderweb hung from some hemlock twigs. The sun shining through it made it dazzle and sparkle like a thousand glittering diamonds.

The undergrowth became thicker, and Dannie noticed that they had left the trail. *Uh, oh,* he thought. *It will never do to get lost in these woods. I'll have to remember always to keep within range of the trail.*

After a while he gave a shout of delight. Just ahead was an overgrown tangle of delicious-looking wild blueberries. They were small but plentiful. He popped one into his mouth and was surprised at its sweetness. Bandit also was fond of the berries, and they both ate their fill, while a pair of blue jays scolded them from a tree. They didn't like others raiding their blueberry patch.

When neither of them could eat another berry, Bandit climbed from Dannie's shoulder onto a low tree branch. Standing on his hind legs, with his comical goggle eyes, he seemed to be intently staring at something through the tree branches. He cocked his head, then turned it from side to side, chirring questioningly.

Dannie couldn't help but laugh at the coon's ridiculous antics. "Are you showing off, you little ham?" he asked, stroking the coon's fur.

Bandit paid him no heed. He really was seeing something. Dannie followed his gaze and then understood. He knew that raccoons are fascinated by bright and shiny objects, anything that sparkles and glitters. There, on a slight bank in the woods, was a heap of old trash.

The sun was dazzling on some old metal objects, tin cans, and junked contraptions. The trash had been left there years earlier, before such dumping in the woods was outlawed. Dannie made a note of the landmarks so he would not lose his way. Then he and Bandit headed straight for the dump.

"What luck!" Dannie cried, when they came closer. He saw how large and interesting the dump appeared to be. Maybe he could find some useful objects to furnish his cabin! Yes, there was an old iron porch rocker, just what he needed!

Then, tossing some trash aside, he unearthed a large agate-ware pot. "Whoopee!" he cried. "Now I can have my corn on the cob!" He pulled out an old rusty, broken-handled shovel. "Say, this will be fine to scoop old dirt and shells out of the cabin!" he said happily.

Bandit, too, was having the time of his life. He had found an old glittering silvery trinket of some sort. Clutching it in his "hands," he rocked back and forth on his heels. Dannie laughed until he was wiping tears, then continued his treasure hunt.

He found an old chipped urn with ornately carved handles, an old dented small round folding table, and an old stove grate. Seeing his pile of collected junk, he told the coon, "We'd better stop now, Bandit. We already have more than we can carry. Later we'll come back and get some more things."

They started off through the thickets. Dannie had his arms loaded high. Bandit followed behind, clutching another shiny medallion he had found.

At their cabin home, Dannie first scrubbed the agate-ware kettle in the spring pool, then proceeded to start a fire. He had gone camping last year with the Boy Scouts and knew all about safety measures to guard against a forest fire. Dannie didn't want a big campfire, just enough to boil a few ears of corn, with no telltale cloud of smoke rising above the tall trees.

After putting down a ring of rocks away from all underbrush, he gathered some dry leaves, grass, and twigs, and small pieces of dry wood. Luckily, he had thought to bring a few books of matches. The fire blazed up brightly as he coaxed it along and fed it larger pieces of wood.

Dannie put the old grate on top of the rocks, and on it the agate pot half full of water from the spring. When the water began to boil merrily, he dropped four ears of the corn carefully into it. Bandit watched, trilling excitedly, fascinated by the flames.

"There, there, little coon, don't get excited," Dannie told his pet. "It won't hurt you if you stay away from it."

When the corn was cooked, Dannie took two handkerchiefs from his satchel to use for potholders. He poured off the water and waited for the corn to cool.

"We're living a life fit for a king;" Dannie gloated to Bandit. "Today we dine on sweet corn, and tomorrow it will be fresh brook trout!"

A few minutes later, when he took his first bite of sweet corn, his heart sank. No butter and no salt! It was a disappointment. For a few minutes, Dannie stared dejectedly at the dying embers.

Then he jumped up, startling Bandit. *The dried beef!* He had almost forgotten that he had brought along some other food. The dried beef was salty, and if he ate it with the corn, the flavor of both would improve. It worked.

Later Dannie lay on the carpet of pine needles under the trees, with Bandit curled beside him. He was still munching sweet corn and dried beef. Dannie was watching the swaying branches overhead and thinking, *That's the best meal I've ever eaten.*

20

Cleaning Up

THE swaying of the hemlock branches lulled them both to sleep. When Dannie awoke a short time later, he decided it was high time to clean the old cabin. Bandit was still curled up beside the minnow pool, fast asleep, so he left him there and got busy.

Taking the old shovel he had found in the dump, Dannie scooped out all the pinecones and walnut shells, then wished for a broom to sweep the floor clean. He thought hard, then came up with the idea of using hemlock branches to sweep the dust and debris out the door. They weren't as good as a broom but still did the job.

When that was done, he filled the old urn with spring water and carried it into the cabin. Using his handkerchief for a cleaning cloth, he first scrubbed the windows inside and out. That made the water so dirty that he had to change it before going over each window again. Then he used small hemlock branches dipped in water to scrub the mantel and the bunks, and finally the hearth and the floor.

It was hard work, what with having to carry in fresh water every five minutes or so, and having no soap. But when he was finished, he was pleased with the results. He was covered with grime and decided to go for a swim while the washed cabin dried out.

First he rinsed out the urn and filled it with fresh spring water again. Then, taking his pocketknife, he cut an armful of ferns growing beside the cabin clearing, arranged them in the urn and set it upon the mantel.

Next Dannie went back to the dump and picked up the other things he had selected. He cleaned the little old folding table, set it up in the middle of the cabin, covered it with one of his spare shirts, and set the agate-ware pot on it. Finally he stepped back to survey his work.

"Yes," he declared with an air of satisfaction, "this is beginning to look like a house. All it needs is some rugs and curtains and a few chairs. Tomorrow we'll root through the dump and see if there is anything else we can use. And I'll clean out the old chimney so I can cook my meals inside instead of outside."

Going out to the pool, he nudged Bandit. "Wake up, Lazybones. We're going to find a swimming hole. I know you'll like that." He felt good, knowing that he had cleaned up the cabin and it was more livable.

As he walked down the sun-dappled path with the coon perched on his shoulder, Dannie heard the wind purring in the pines. He looked into the green depths and spied two red squirrels chasing each other around the trunk of a big sycamore tree. "There's always something new and interesting to see in the woods, Bandit," Dannie reflected to his pet.

As if to prove his words true, just at that moment a young wild turkey, with a quick flapping of wings, rose out of the brush. It sailed into the air, then plunged downward again and dived into a thicket.

"See, Bandit," Dannie went on, "no wonder coons like it best in the woods." A side branch off the trail took them down over a hillside. He heard a sound coming from a lower spot and recognized it as falling water. Dannie knew he had not seen this before, so he left the main trail.

Again he took careful notice of landmarks so he wouldn't get lost. What he had heard was just a small rushing, tumbling, mountain stream that collected in a little pool among rocks, halfway down the slope. Then it cascaded over a waterfall, and again collected in a larger pool, before it flowed on down into the shallow creek in the valley.

Dannie set Bandit on a rock, took off his shirt, then took a plunge into the invigorating water in the larger pool. "Brrrr! Spring water!" he cried. Shivering, breathless, and gasping, he climbed out onto the rock beside Bandit. A moment later, he plunged in again. There was something exhilarating about swimming in such cold water, even though it nearly took his breath away.

Seeing what fun Dannie was having, Bandit soon joined him there. Together they splashed happily in the pool, sometimes under the waterfall, letting the cold bracing water massage their backs and shoulders. They would dive back into the deepest part until they were tired, and then they happily sunned themselves on the rock.

Now Dannie felt squeaky clean. The empty feeling in the pit of his stomach told him that it was nearing suppertime, but he felt too lazy to move. Then, not ten feet away, a rustling of the grasses caught his attention. He sat bolt upright, half expecting to see a bobcat come creeping out.

Instead, when the grasses parted, there stood a half-grown fawn, his big limpid unblinking brown eyes looking straight at Dannie without a trace of fear. The fawn took a few steps toward him, and Dannie noticed that he had a decided limp in his one leg, just like Ivor's fawn had.

"Yes, it is Ivor and Helga's little fawn!" he whispered. He hardly dared to breathe for fear of scaring the fawn away. Dannie stared transfixed, not even wanting to move, but the fawn didn't seem to show any fear. They gazed at each other for a long moment. For some strange reason, Dannie felt his eyes filling with tears.

Then, with a quavering little bleat, the fawn jumped back into the grasses and bounded away. A sudden feeling of homesickness engulfed Dannie. He enjoyed camping in the hemlock woods, but now he felt a tugging to go back to civilization. Here, there was no one to talk with, no one to criticize, and no one even to ignore.

In spite of himself, Dannie had to smile. Then, for the first time since his dad had left, he began to realize what a difficult and unreasonable person he had been, and he felt ashamed. *When I go back,* he resolved, *I won't be that way anymore.*

Deep in thought, he and Bandit slowly made their way to the cabin. As he mulled things over in his mind, he prepared a supper of the last of the sweet corn, dried beef, and freshly picked blueberries.

After supper, Dannie got his fishing line and headed for the creek. Still absorbed in thought, he sat on the creek bank, waiting for a nibble on his line. Bandit waded in the shallow water, feeling for crayfish. After a while, the sun began to set in a golden bank of clouds beneath the next ridge of green treetops.

They returned to the cabin, tying their meager catch of a few small sunnies (bluegills) securely into the spring pool beside the cabin. He grabbed the rusty old rocker from the dump and pulled it up to the door of the cabin.

Dannie sat with Bandit on his knee, watching the twilight descend into the hemlocks and pines, hearing night insects calling and forest folks rustling in the thickets. The silvery moon was rising, visible through a gap in a big pine. He heard the twittery notes of a late songbird as it hopped from branch to branch.

From far across the woods came the spine-chilling but sad and lonely wail that Dannie had heard before. It was the long-drawn-out "Awa–ooooh–ooh–awa–ooooo" howl of Ivor's wolf. The eerie sound pricked at the back of Dannie's knees and the soles of his feet. It sent a sudden shiver through him.

Bandit, too, sensed the fear and edged closer to Dannie, chirring in that questioning way of his.

"Time for bed, Bandit." Dannie tried to sound brave, but his voice quivered a bit. "Tomorrow morning it will be better again."

21

Something Strange

THE next Sunday was a no-church day in their district. In the afternoon Nancy and Sally decided to take a walk through Hemlock Hill and to go on to visit Ivor and Helga, too. Omar and Andrew had a supper invitation and were going to a singing in another district, so they weren't interested in going along.

They headed up the trail and entered the shadowy hemlock woods. As they strolled along, Nancy exclaimed, "Just think, Sally, in a little more than a year from now, you'll be *rumschpringing* (going with the young folks)! Can you believe it?"

"Hmph! It won't be much fun going without you along!" Sally pouted. "I can hardly stand it that you'll have to wait nine months longer to turn sixteen. I have half a notion just to wait until you're allowed to go, too."

"I'll believe that when I see it!" Nancy said, laughing. "Wherever you go, you have no trouble making friends. You'll probably be half married before I even start *rumschpringing*."

"Half married!" Sally scoffed, then began to giggle. "There's no such thing."

"Well, anyway, going steady, then. Say, I sure hope Ivor and Helga are home after our long walk. At least it's cool here under the hemlocks."

"We'll come to the first spring soon," Sally replied. "I can't wait to drink some spring water with mint leaves. That taste sure beats all."

"Let's stop at the little cabin, too," Nancy suggested. "Ever since I first saw it, I've wanted to explore some more. It's too bad Dannie can't be along today. I sure wonder how Joe and Arie are making out with him. Omar and I miss him a lot."

"Well, I think he'll be all right as long as he has that little coon of his." Sally stopped to take deep breaths of the hemlock-scented air. She held up a hand. "Listen! Isn't that a pine siskin I hear?" She sank down on a bed of emerald green moss.

Nancy plopped down beside her, on a soft bed of pine needles. "I don't know. I've never heard one. But I think I hear a chickadee."

A twig snapped in a nearby thicket, then something crashed through the underbrush. The girls jumped to their feet. "Wh–what was that?" Sally asked shakily. "Ivor's wolf?"

"I hope not," Nancy declared. "Let's go on before we lose courage."

Coming to the little cabin, the girls tried the door, but found it barred. "That's strange," Sally muttered. "It was never locked before. Let's peek in the window." A moment later she drew back, stifling a scream.

"What is it?" Nancy asked fearfully.

"It was an animal, streaking across the room," Sally said shakily.

"A black-and-gray streak, but bigger than a rat or a squirrel. Say, let's get out of here!"

The girls hurried on up the trail. A short time later, they had another scare as they heard the howl of Ivor's wolf echoing through the woods. So they gave a sigh of relief when they reached the safe haven of Ivor and Helga's shady porch. There the old couple sat and rocked, with the wolf stretched out between them.

"Good afternoon! Come and take seats!" Helga and Ivor greeted the girls warmly.

"We're right glad to see you. You came at the right time," Ivor told them. "Helga just finished reading an interesting storybook to me, as gripping as they come. Would you like me to tell you what it's about?"

"Please do!" Sally begged, settling down on the bench. "I love your stories." Nancy felt the same way.

"The title of the book is *Big Smoke Mountain,* by Lewis B. Miller," Ivor told them. "I'll give you a little sample. But I don't want to rob you of the thrill and suspense of reading the book yourselves sometime."

He settled back into his rocker and began. "Two boys named Zally and Oscar one day went out to gather pecans. Four Comanche braves came riding out of the brush, killed the dogs with their arrows, and captured the boys. They seated each of them behind a mounted brave and rode off.

"The boys were scared and had little hope of escaping. At night, one brave used an end of a long buffalo-hide rope to tie Zally's feet together, and tied Oscar's feet together with the other end. The brave lay down on the middle of the rope.

"During the night, Zally remembered that he still had his pocketknife. Without waking the brave, he cut himself loose, then cut Oscar loose, too. They quietly crawled away and had nearly made it to safety when one of the horses saw them and snorted. This woke the captors, and the chase was on.

"The boys were soon recaptured, managed to escape again, and were captured a third time. That night they were securely tied to trees just outside the camp. Their backs were against the trunks, ankles fastened together with buffalo-hide ropes, and hands pulled in back of the tree and tightly bound together with buckskin thongs.

"They wondered if this was their last night on earth. There didn't seem to be any way for them to escape. But during the night it rained. The wet buckskin cords stretched, so they got their hands free and untied their ankles."

Ivor laughed softly to himself. "The two boys were hoofing it again. This time they got away and traveled up into Big Smoke Mountain. There they found shelter in a cave and then built a snug rock house with a fireplace. They killed a bear, and one boy used its skin for a coat. For the other boy, they found the skin of a buffalo calf that wolves had killed.

"They even tamed a young wolf for a pet, just like I did. I won't tell you what else happened to them, before they got back to their families. But I'm sure that story is worth reading if you like adventure." Ivor handed the book to Nancy. "Here, take it along for Omar to read. I know he'd like it."

Helga brought them some refreshing mint tea again, with slices of a cake she called bannocks. It was delicious! The girls soon thanked Ivor and Helga for their hospitality and prepared to leave.

"Say, girls, I just happened to think of something," Ivor said. "Is anything going on over in the hemlock woods? I've seen a thin column of smoke there several times these past few days, and my wolf seems to sense something amiss over there. He's been howling more of late, as if serenading someone or something suspicious."

Nancy and Sally exchanged worried glances. "We came through there on our way over," Nancy told him. "The old cabin door was locked. When Sally peeked in the window, she saw a gray-and-black animal running."

"Yes, and just before that, we heard twigs snapping and something crashing through the underbrush," Sally added. "Has your wolf been up there this afternoon?"

"No, ma'am, he hasn't." Ivor was sure of it. "But I'm going up there to investigate. Do you mind if I walk with you girls?"

"Mind!" Sally cried. "It will be a relief to have you along. I was secretly thinking that maybe we should go home by the road, the long way round. But I didn't want Nancy to know how scared I was."

"Well, at least it's a comfort to know that there is no danger of meeting any Comanche braves," Nancy said. "And I'm sure we'll be safe with a wolf along for protection."

Thus it happened that the two girls, the old man, and a huge timber wolf climbed the trail up through the hemlock woods.

22

Backtracking

WITH Bandit on his shoulder, Dannie had been wandering aimlessly through the shadowy, piney woods on Sunday afternoon. He was longing for human companionship and thinking wistfully of his friends.

Time hung heavy on his hands. He found out that a boy could spend only so much time fishing and hiking and daydreaming, until he tired of it. Dannie wondered why Bandit spent so much of his time sleeping in the daytime. Had he found some way to get out of the cabin and roam the woods at night while Dannie slept?

Presently Dannie thought he heard voices, and he stopped in his tracks. A flash of blue through the sun-dappled foliage caught his attention. He crept closer to see what it was. A minute later he gasped. Nancy and Sally came into full view, walking along the trail and visiting as they walked.

From behind a bush, Dannie watched as they seated themselves on the forest floor, and he tried to stand as quiet as possible, his heart racing. He shifted his weight, then crack! A twig broke under his foot. Quick as a flash, he threw himself down, rolled over a small knob, and then hightailed it into a thicket of honeysuckle vines.

Heart pounding, he waited to hear if the girls were following him. All remained quiet, so he ran off, out of the brambles. He crawled through the underbrush and took a roundabout way to the cabin. Bandit was trilling excitedly again. Dannie set him on the bunk and quickly barred the door.

Crawling under the bunk, he pulled the hemlock branches over himself and Bandit, and waited. A short time later, he heard voices. The girls were at the door. Before he could stop him, Bandit slipped from Dannie's arms and rushed out from under the hemlocks and over to the door, chirring questioningly.

"Come back!" Dannie called, in a hoarse whisper. "Bandit!"

The little raccoon stood there, looking bewildered. Finally he understood and dashed back across the room to his master. Dannie waited until all was quiet and he was sure the girls had left. Then he got busy.

Unlocking the door, he quickly dragged out the hemlock boughs and hid them in the brush. He carried out the rusty table, the urn, the pot, his satchel and fishing line, along with the old rocker. Dannie hid them all in the woods, a safe distance from the cabin. He would leave no trace and no trail!

By the time Ivor and the girls arrived several hours later, nothing was amiss. Dannie and Bandit were over on the other side of the mountain, by the waterfall.

This time, when the girls tried the cabin door, it opened immediately, and the three cautiously stepped inside. "Nobody here now, but there has been recently," Ivor declared. "See how Wolf sniffs out the corners."

"Yes, and it seems to be cleaned up already," Nancy observed.

"Oooooh! What if it's an escaped prisoner, using this as a hideaway?" Sally said with a shiver. "Nancy, you'd better sleep over at our house tonight, since Omar will be at the singing till late. I couldn't bear to think of you over here all alone until he comes."

Nancy nodded. "That's a good idea. I guess I will."

"Now girls, I didn't mean to frighten you," Ivor said. "I don't think there's a thing to worry about. My wolf here is real keen. If he would think there's danger nearby, he'd let us know. It's quite safe for you to go on home."

Nevertheless, after the girls had gone, Ivor decided to search the woods some more with his wolf. Meanwhile, across the hill, Dannie lay on his back, resting on a bed of pine needles, with his hands cupped behind his head. He was staring up into the hemlock boughs, deep in thought. As usual, Bandit was curled up by his side.

The sound of the waterfall was soothing, but Dannie's thoughts were troubling. Maybe he should just go back to Omar and Nancy now. Surely it wouldn't be too hard to think up some story to explain away this past week. Maybe he could say he had gone to visit a friend and lost his way or something similar.

On the other hand, Dannie didn't want to tell a lie. Somewhere, deep inside, he had a real longing to do better, to live a different life, free from bitterness, anger, and rebellion.

He rolled over on his stomach and watched the clear, sparkling water tumbling down over the rocks. Dannie pondered the fact that his attitude was changing. From now on, he really wanted to head in the right direction, instead of making all kinds of trouble for those who tried to help him.

Dannie no longer felt the need to be alone all the time. He had gotten his fill of that here in the cabin hideaway among the hemlocks. No longer did he feel afraid of getting close to others, of allowing himself to love them.

He decided that he could accept whatever his dad had done, even if it didn't seem fair. He would choose to forgive him and bravely go on, making the best of his circumstances. Having made this decision, a burden seemed to roll off Dannie's back.

"We're going home now, Bandit!" he said cheerfully to the little coon. "I'll tell Omar everything, and all will be fair and square between us again. I know it will. Let's go! Nancy might make some of her fluffy mashed potatoes, meatloaf, and vegetables for supper. It's been a long time since I've had a real meal, with fresh corn on the cob—"

He stopped short. Thinking of sweet corn reminded Dannie of how Bandit was likely to raid any patch of ripe corn—and of something else he'd practically forgotten. What if the tomcat had rabies? Bandit was not out of danger yet. He might still lose his life.

Dannie threw himself back down on the bank dejectedly. "No, Bandit," he said sadly. "We can't go back yet." A tear began to roll down over Dannie's cheek, but he angrily brushed it away.

Suddenly Dannie was startled by a deep-throated growl coming from the nearby wild alder thicket. He jumped to his feet, ready to run. Slowly the bushes parted, revealing the huge, shaggy head of Ivor's wolf. His jade-green slanted eyes looked more inquisitive than ferocious. A few steps behind him came Ivor, around the thicket instead of through it.

"Well, well, if it isn't Dannie boy and the little coon," Ivor's friendly booming voice rang out. Seeing traces of recent tears on Dannie's cheeks, he said kindly, "There now, boy, won't you tell me what the trouble is? It can't be so very bad."

Before long Dannie was pouring out the whole story to the kindhearted old man. He told about loving his pet coon, and the rabies scare from the mean old tomcat. Dannie explained why he had run away and why he wanted to go back.

"Good for you, Dannie," Ivor said warmly. "You've

made the right decision. And I can reassure you that my old tomcat doesn't have rabies. He's had a spite for coons ever since he was old enough to catch mice, that's all. I really wondered what become of him, until Omar told me.

"You know, though, that Bandit won't be happy as a farm pet forever. When the cold weather comes, nothing will make him happier than to find a big old partly hollow tree in the woods. He needs a tree with a hollowed-out nest in it, lined with soft leaves. The coon will spend most of his time sleeping in it, only coming down to eat now and then.

"Then next spring, he'll be restless and cranky and unreasonable if he can't have his way. He'll want to have a life of his own, in the woods with other coon friends. But you'll always have the memory of this summer when you were Bandit's best friend.

"Come, Dannie. Helga's making supper, and she has plenty enough for you, too, I'm sure. You can spend the night with us, and tomorrow I'll take you home. You have some wonderful friends there in the Petersheim family. I hope you appreciate them and what they're doing for you."

That night as Dannie lay in the big four-poster bed in Ivor and Helga's spare room, he thought over what Ivor had said. *Yes, it is true, the Petersheims are a mighty nice family,* he mused. *I'm sorry for how cranky I was and the mischief I did.*

Again he resolved, *From now on, I'll be different. When Bandit wants to leave me, I'll ask for another chance to have a puppy. I know now that I was hurt-*

ing myself more than anyone else by being so contrary.

As Dannie drifted off to dreamland, there was a smile on his face. He was happier than he had been for a long, long time.

23

Church Sunday

AFTER his hideout experience in the hemlock woods, Dannie was like a different boy. He was up before dawn every morning, with the crowing of the roosters, ready to help Omar with the chores. The early sweet corn was over. There was a lapse of several weeks until the next batch was ready, so Bandit was free for a while.

With Jacob's help, Omar had been building calf pens in the back of the barn. At last the barn was ready for seventy-five newborn veal calves. It was an exciting time for Omar, Nancy, and Dannie when the cattle trucks arrived. The bawling calves were unloaded into "the calf barn," as they started calling it now.

There was a day's work ahead. They had to tie them in the proper pens. Then came the hardest job of all, teaching them to drink out of a bucket. The calves had no idea how to do that since they had just been taken from their mamas.

Omar had no electric veal-feed mixer. To prepare milk replacer for so many calves by hand would have been quite a job. So they used a wringer washing machine run by a gas engine and let its agitator mix the milk replacer.

In front of each calf was a wooden frame with a round opening just the size of a bucket. The plastic calf buckets were set in the openings so the calves couldn't butt the buckets and spill the milk replacer.

Nancy had looked forward to helping with the calves, but whew! So many cute bawling, wooly black-and-white calves at once were nearly too much. Omar showed Dannie how to dip a finger into the milk mixture, get the calf started sucking his finger, and then lower his hand into the milk. If the calf was smart, it caught on after awhile and kept on drinking.

Some of the calves were slow learners. Dannie and the others would struggle to teach one such calf for fifteen or twenty minutes, and then it was the same thing over again at the next feeding.

After a few days, all of the calves caught on and began to drink as soon as the bucket was put into the holder. They happily slapped their tails from side to side while they drank.

Omar told Nancy and Dannie to watch for calf scours, a common ailment of such young calves. He wanted to give the proper treatment before it was too late to save the calf.

Dannie pitched in and helped all he could. That was a blessing as summer wore on. Omar had planted some acres for produce, too. Cantaloupes were just beginning to ripen. Next would be watermelons. They picked wagonloads of the fruits daily and took them to the produce auction four miles away. Andrew and Sally came over to help, and Jacob gave a hand whenever he could, too.

When she woke one Sunday morning, Nancy was genuinely glad to realize that it was a day of rest instead of a workday. Church would be at the Fisher's place today. But then, oh, no! The thought struck her that those bawling calves had to be fed today as well as any other day. That meant several hours of work in the morning and again in the evening. She groaned but jumped out of bed in a hurry.

Dannie was already up, and she heard him whistling as he headed for the calf barn. It gave her a good feeling inside to hear it, glad that the boy's sulleness was gone. It really was an answer to prayer, as Mamm had written in her last letter.

Omar had the washing-machine mixer going already when Nancy stepped into the barn. Dannie was setting the buckets of milk replacer in front of the calves, who were impatiently dancing around in their stalls as if half starved.

"Good morning!" Omar greeted her, above the noise of the mixer engine. "It's going to be a beautiful day—and lovely for volleyball at the Fishers' place this afternoon. Then we'll come home to do chores. This evening we young people have the singing at the Fishers."

"I wish I'd be old enough to go with the youth," Nancy sighed. "This time, I think I'll go anyhow. Since it's at her place, Sally has invited me. We could sit in a corner, where no one would notice us."

Omar looked doubtful. "You'd better ask Mary about that," he cautioned. "Next Dannie would want to go, too."

Sometimes it was up to Omar to make decisions in place of their parents, and he was glad for counsel from his sister Mary.

Just as they expected, it was hurry, hurry, hurry all morning. A boisterous calf somehow managed to get out of its pen. It ran out the barn door before anyone could stop it. The calf led the three of them on a merry chase around the barnyard. It nearly headed out toward the pond before Omar managed to catch it and carry it back to its pen.

Then there were all those buckets to wash yet, too. By the time they were finally ready for church, it was later than they wanted it to be. They arrived among the last of the carriages and were almost breathless when they had rushed to the house.

Nancy gratefully sank down on the backless bench beside Sally in the Fisher's basement where the services were to be held. She felt as if she had already done a day's work. Sally flashed her a welcoming smile.

My, it feels good to sit down, Nancy thought, wishing she could have come early enough to visit awhile with Sally and the other girls before church. *I just hope I won't doze off.*

The weather was extra warm. The basement doors had been left open for ventilation.

Jacob, the *Vorsinger* (song leader), was beginning the familiar, slow tune. Nancy let herself relax as his deep, melodious voice rose and fell in a solo for a few notes until with one accord the others heartily joined in.

When the first minister stood to speak, Nancy heard a stir of commotion among the boys. She stretched her neck to see what was up. Dannie was sitting quietly with bowed head, but there were movements and snickering among the boys in the same row. Nancy saw a streak of black-and-gray. The next moment, Bandit jumped up on Dannie's knee, then climbed onto his shoulder and snuggled down contentedly. At last he was where he wanted to be.

Nancy nearly gasped aloud. The preacher was looking straight at Dannie, but Dannie neither moved nor raised his head. Soon all was quiet again, and the preacher began to speak. There was no danger of Nancy dozing off now, as she thought, *Why doesn't Dannie take Bandit outside?* Bandit must have thought he was okay where he was, for he appeared to have fallen asleep.

The coon slept till church was over. Then Dannie carried him outside, under the big shade tree in the front yard. They were surrounded by a group of boys, all wanting to pet and hold Bandit. Most of them were a bit envious but admiring, and Dannie found himself and his pet the center of attention. Before this Sunday, he had always felt himself an outsider, but now at last he felt like one of them.

The worship service at Fisher's place was followed by the usual church fellowship meal. In the afternoon, the young people played volleyball till late afternoon, when it was time for them to go home and do chores.

That evening, after the calves were fed again, Bandit even got to attend his first singing. Mary gave permission for Nancy and Dannie to go along—"just until the singing part is over, of course." She and Jacob and Nancy Ann were going, too.

At the singing, Bandit again perched on Dannie's shoulder and attracted a lot of attention. Andrew tossed him a piece of toffee candy. Bandit, chirring happily, carefully removed the paper with his humanlike hands, then popped it into his mouth and began to chew on it. He looked so comical and happy that everyone had to laugh at the expression on his face.

After singing for a while, the young people relaxed and started chatting and laughing. That was when Nancy and Dannie walked to Jacob's place with Mary, Jacob, and Nancy Ann. There they would wait for Omar to pick them up with his horse and buggy.

In the warm summer evening, Nancy felt happy and at peace. She wondered if Omar would find an *Aldi* (girlfriend) soon. Then she realized that she couldn't feel as delighted about the idea as she once had. After all, when he got married, she would have to leave Summerville and Hemlock Hill Homestead.

Nancy liked the community and the neighborhood, and she liked keeping house for Omar. Someday she wanted to have a permanent home here, too. She remembered that not so long ago she had thought she would never leave Whispering Brook Farm. But now her affections had shifted to Summerville.

24

Good Neighbors

SUMMER'S warm days gradually gave way to cooler fall weather. Flocks of wild geese winged their way southward, and leafy trees displayed colorful autumn foliage. At Hemlock Hill Homestead, Nancy and Omar were gathering hickory nuts, shellbarks, and pecans by the basketful.

Dannie was back at Whispering Brook Farm, cooperating in school, and making a new name for himself. Omar and Nancy were busy with the harvesting all fall. Then in early November, winter arrived before they were ready for it, dumping a foot of snow over the countryside. It was bitterly cold for a few days afterward.

"Brrr! This kitchen is downright chilly!" Nancy told

herself the morning after the storm. She was pulling on a sweater as she boiled some water on the gas stove to make herself some hot chocolate.

"Since we don't have a wood-burning cookstove, I wonder how well we'll be able to heat the place this winter with only the old coal furnace in the basement. Maybe I should start a fire in the fireplace, too."

She was alone for the day. Omar had gone to a livestock auction with Jacob and would not be back until mid-afternoon. Mary had gone shopping with a vanload of other mothers. All the neighbors had been glad to see the snowplow opening the roads early that morning.

As she sipped from her cup, Nancy gazed admiringly out the window. She saw snow-blanketed fields and the picturesque pine boughs laden with soft, fluffy heaps of snow. The dark green of the hemlocks and the white of the snow made a lovely contrast. The sky was an azure blue, and the bright sunshine dazzled and sparkled on the glittering drifts.

The white birches were stark and bare against their background of evergreens, accenting their beauty. The big pond had frozen over a short time before it snowed. It was not quite safe yet for them to skate on it, but the young people hoped to be able to have a skating party soon. Just now she could hardly even tell where the pond was, since the snow had drifted over it so much.

Suddenly Nancy gasped. There, trotting along in the field beside the pond, was a horse. It was none other than Beauty, Omar's prize steed. He was happily capering and prancing in the snow, his mane and tail flying in the wind. Beauty was making the most of his exhilarating new freedom in the snowy outdoors.

The horse stopped and began to paw at the snow, making it fly, trying to find grass underneath. Then he gave up. Wild and free and upheaded, he broke into a gallop, made a neat turn, and looped back, heading straight for the deep end of the pond.

"Stop, Beauty!" cried Nancy, in the kitchen. But Beauty, unaware of the danger, ran out onto the snow-covered ice. Then, as if suddenly sensing the danger, he stopped in his tracks.

There was a sharp crack, and Nancy quickly covered her face with her hands, unable to watch him disappear beneath the ice. When she looked again, she could see nothing of the horse, only a big area of open water with floating pieces of ice.

For a few moments, Nancy stood as if turned to stone, then sprang into action. She grabbed her jacket and kerchief and pulled on her boots. Then she ran to the barn, threw the harness on Dandy, and with trembling hands hitched him to the pony cart. She dared not so much as glance toward the pond.

Nancy urged the pony into a fast trot. The lane was open because Omar had used the workhorses to scrape it this morning before he left. "Come on, Dandy, faster, faster," Nancy urged. "*Ach mei* (oh, my), we must save Beauty!"

How she hoped that either Andrew or his dad would be at home. *What, oh what will I do if they aren't there?*

Dandy did his best. The trees along the lane whizzed by, and they barely made the turn into Fishers' drive. In a cloud of snow spray, Nancy drove up to the door of the harness shop and yanked open the door. She was hoping against hope that help would be there and that it would not be too late for Beauty.

"Anybody home? Help! Help!" she cried breathlessly.

A moment later an astonished Andrew appeared from the back of the shop. "What's wrong?" he asked, wild-eyed. "Is somebody hurt?"

"It's Beauty, our horse," Nancy gasped. "He broke through the ice in the deepest part of the pond, and I'm afraid he'll drown. Can't you do something?"

Andrew disappeared, and a moment later came back, carrying an ax and a coil of rope.

"Let's go," he cried, hopping onto the pony cart. "We'll see what we can do."

Dandy was still fired up to go, and a short time later they were heading in Omar's lane.

"I'm sure it was my fault that Beauty got out of his stall," Nancy mourned. "I was the last one in the barn this morning. Omar was in a hurry, and I told him I'd finish. *Ach, guck* (oh, look)! There's Beauty swimming in the open water," Nancy cried excitedly.

They were now bumping over snow and ice in the field, and Dandy had to work hard to pull the cart. Beauty's head was still above water, but all around him was snow-covered ice. He was becoming tired from thrashing around, but there was no way he could get out by himself.

Andrew quickly jumped off the cart at the pond's edge, tied the rope around his waist, and gave the other end to Nancy. "Now we'll see if the ice is strong enough to hold me. If I break in, pull me to safety."

He began to chop a path through the ice, staying

far enough away so he wouldn't slide in himself. Further and farther out he went with his chopped path, closer and closer to the struggling Beauty.

Nancy's lips were moving in prayer: "Oh, please, don't let Andrew break in, too," she said over and over. "Let the ice hold." Finally Andrew was near enough to fasten the end of the rope to Beauty's halter. Slowly he made his way back to the shore, tugging at the rope every now and then to keep Beauty following him.

Nancy was almost holding her breath, fearing Andrew would break through before he made the bank. With a sigh of relief, she watched Andrew crawl out to safety. Then Beauty sprang up onto the bank, shaking himself, with water and ice droplets flying off his back in all directions. "Thank-you, thank-you!" she whispered. Oh, what a good feeling!

Andrew led Beauty into the warmth of the barn, then rubbed him down well and covered him with two stable blankets. Nancy unhitched Dandy and put him into his stable.

"Come on in, then," Nancy called to Andrew. "I'll make some more hot chocolate."

"Sounds good," Andrew agreed.

"I just wish it were a bit warmer in here," Nancy lamented, when they entered the kitchen. "I guess I should start a fire in the fireplace, but I don't think Omar has cleaned out the chimney."

"Let me do it," Andrew offered. "It will only take a few minutes—I know where the ladder is."

A short time later, Andrew came back. "It's a good

thing you didn't start a fire before I checked it out. An old chimney swift's nest was up there. Your kitchen would have filled with smoke pretty fast. The chimney's open now."

Nancy had the kindling ready, and a cheerful blaze soon crackled on the hearth. The kitchen began filling with the cozy warmth of apple wood that had been saved for just this purpose.

As the two sat by the fire and sipped mugs of hot chocolate, Nancy had a deep feeling of gratefulness. Good neighbors were such a blessing, willing to drop everything to come and help when the need arose.

"How can I ever thank you enough?" Nancy asked Andrew. "Oh, how awful I'd be feeling if Beauty had drowned, and it was my fault!"

"I was happy to help," Andrew assured her. "Who knows? You may have to come to our aid sometime. That's what good neighbors are for."

"Well, I'm so glad you were here to rescue Beauty."

"Any time! Now don't forget to take those blankets off Beauty in about an hour, or he'll get too hot in the stable."

After Andrew had left, Nancy sat for awhile, deep in thought, mostly about Andrew. *When did he change?* she wondered. *Come to think of it, I haven't heard him tease someone or act biggety for ages.*

Now he sure is willing to help others. He has grown up right before my eyes, and I haven't noticed until now. I guess it's true what Jacob said, "Andrew is making a real man out of himself."

25

Family

THE winter passed by swiftly. The weather cooperated beautifully to make plenty of smooth ice on the pond. Omar and Andrew scraped and brushed the snow off the ice, and the young people had one skating party after the other, quite to their heart's content.

At Christmastime, the youths went caroling, riding on big sleighs pulled by plodding workhorses, with merrily jingling bells attached to the harnesses. There were sledding parties, too, and for Nancy and Sally, quilting bees and gatherings to knot comforters.

When spring arrived, there was another nursemaid job for Nancy, this time at Mary and Jacob's house— a cute little brother for Nancy Ann.

"My, what a *schnuck Buppeli* (cute baby)!" Nancy

said admiringly, when she saw the new bundle in Mary's arms. "A head full of dark hair and a tiny up-turned nose! Do you think Nancy Ann will give me a chance to hold him sometimes, too?"

"Maybe like now, when she's napping," Mary said wryly. "She's so possessive with him. She'll have to learn to share, that's one sure thing."

Jacob came in with a pail full of milk to strain. "We decided to wait to name him until you get here. Do you have any special admirers you'd like to name the baby after?"

Nancy wrinkled her nose. "How would I know? I think Jacob would be as good a name as any—Jacob Junior."

Jacob shook his head. "Not the oldest boy. I hope to have at least half a dozen. There should be plenty of time for a junior later. How about Elmer?"

That suited Mary fine, and so the boy became Elmer. Nancy was glad Jacob didn't pursue the subject of her admirers any further.

Nancy enjoyed every minute of her two-week job of working for Mary. Nancy Ann was a sweet little girl, and caring for the baby was almost like playing with a doll used to be. But baby Elmer now was a real live, soft, warm, cuddly, huggable little bundle. Nancy and Nancy Ann thought that holding him was the sweetest job in the world.

On the last day of Nancy's stay at Jacob's place, Sally came over with her noodle maker to help Nancy make several batches of homemade noodles. They filled a big bowl with flour, made a well in it, and added egg yolks. The dough had to be mixed and kneaded for a long time, until it was exactly firm enough.

"It seems like a long time since we spent a day together like this," Nancy said, shaping a mound of yellow dough with her hands. Nancy Ann was at her elbow, ready to turn the handle of the noodle maker.

"Sure does," Sally agreed. "I do believe it's all of three weeks. If the day ever comes that you move back home, I'll be like a lost puppy. The same friendship holds with Andrew and Omar, too, even though Omar is older."

She deftly fed the portion of dough into the noodle maker, first at a thick setting, then very thin, and finally she put a piece through to be sliced in thin strands to show Nancy Ann what they would look like.

"I think Omar is here to stay," Nancy stated. "I do wonder, though, when he is going to get himself an *Aldi* (girlfriend)."

"Good things take time," Sally quipped lightly.

Mary came into the kitchen, holding baby Elmer. "I think I just heard a vehicle drive in." She went over to the window, then gasped. "Why, it's a van—and Mamm and Daed and the whole family are along," she cried joyously. "What a nice surprise! Now we'll have a lot of help with the noodle making."

Susie and Lydia hurried in, eager to see their new nephew, followed by Mamm. They all crowded around the new baby, oohing and aahing over him.

"Just think," Mary told them, "how very tiny Nancy

Ann must have been. By now, Elmer is over twice as big as she was at the same age."

One thing everyone agreed on was that baby Elmer looked a lot like his dad and was a fine, large, healthy baby. Dad and the boys were coming in and wanted to see the new little chap, too.

Nancy stared at Dannie. She could hardly believe how much he had grown. Why, he didn't seem like the same boy! He had been a rather thin, pale boy last summer. Now he was sturdy, already getting tanned by the spring sun, and healthy looking—as hearty and rosy-cheeked as her brothers.

When the menfolk had trooped outside again, she asked, "Mamm, how is Dannie behaving this past while? He looks so relaxed and healthy."

Mom nodded. "He's sure not the same boy that he was when he first came to live with us. There's just nothing we can say by way of complaining about him now. Dannie's doing very well, is a good worker, and he's quite good-natured, too. Isn't it amazing?

"Last month his dad came back for him. He's taken a house in town, and he wanted Dannie to come and live with him. But Dannie has chosen to stay with us. We aren't planning to adopt him, but he's welcome to call our place his home as long as he chooses to do so.

"Dannie wants to come out here and live with you and Omar again this summer, though. He plans to camp out in the little cabin on Hemlock Hill again and visit Ivor and Helga."

"We'll be looking forward to it." Nancy was glad to

hear that news. "What has become of his little coon?"

Mom chuckled. "Little! That raccoon, when he came back for a few days this spring, weighed all of fifteen pounds. He's gone for good now, to the woodland back of your Whispering Brook. Bandit is well able to fend for himself. I sure hope he won't mess with our sweet corn patch this summer."

Nancy's mom helped to prepare a good dinner, including freshly made homemade noodles. Joe, Arie, and little Michael Lee came for dinner, too, and Omar, of course.

As the men were washing up, Sally told Nancy in an undertone, "This is a real family gathering for you. I feel like I'm the only onion in the petunia patch. I think I'd better go on home."

Mom overheard and turned to Sally. "Please stay. We're so glad to have your help with the noodles, and we don't want to make you feel unwelcome."

She was thinking something more that she did not say: *Sally is such a nice girl, fitting in so well with the rest of the family.*

Nancy told Sally, "You said that wrong. You meant that you're the only petunia in the onion patch, didn't you? Boohoo! Boohoo!"

Both girls began to giggle. Omar, hearing their giggles as the family gathered at the table, noticed that Sally was there, and he was glad of it.

26

The Picnic

ANOTHER year passed. Nancy and Sally were now both regularly going to the singings with the youths. They had made their applications to join the church and be baptized, just as Omar and Andrew had done earlier.

One evening as Nancy brought their lone milk cow up from the fragrant, buttercup-filled meadow for the evening milking, Omar met her at the gate. "Ah, Nancy, I—I guess I'd better tell you something before someone else does."

Nancy eyed him keenly, waiting for him to go on. What did he have up his sleeve now? As he was hesitating, she watched a pair of barn swallows swoop out of the open barn door, glide low overhead, and sweep up again in a graceful arch.

"I—I'm going to take a girl home from the singing on Sunday night. I'm sure you can come home with Andrew."

Nancy caught her breath. So Omar had found himself an *Aldi* at last.

Finding herself at a loss for words, she merely said, "Yes, I suppose I can come home with Sally and Andrew. Who—?"

Andrew shook his head, hiding a grin. "Nope, Sally will be going with me."

Nancy gasped. "*Was in die Welt* (what in the world)? I can't believe it! That's just like you, keeping it a secret that you were waiting for Sally all this time."

"I'm not the only one who has secrets," Omar replied.

"Ya well, then I guess it's good-bye, Sally," Nancy said, trying her best to sound doleful.

"What do you mean, 'good-bye, Sally'?" Omar sounded a trifle hurt. "I think it should be 'hello, Sally.'"

"Well, yes, hello to Sally as a future sister-in-law, but good-bye to Sally as my buddy after singings. But anyway, I am very happy for you. Sally is so lively that every minute with her seems like an adventure. But I'm curious. Have you really been planning this for a long time already?"

Omar nodded. "Ever since that day she swallowed a pin, remember? That was the first that I realized that I wanted her."

"Hmm," Nancy said a trifle mischievously, a smile

tugging at the corners of her mouth. "I wonder if she did that on purpose. I'll have to keep that in mind. Maybe it would work for me, too." She couldn't resist a bit of teasing.

"You won't need to bother, I can assure you," Omar said with a knowing smile. "But let's get that cow milked before I give away any more secrets."

Brother and sister sat on their milk stools, one on each side of the cow, and squirted the milk into the same bucket. Nancy couldn't help adding, "Now I understand what that whistle was about when you saw Sally trying on that new dress."

"Ya, well, it took you a while to figure that out," replied Omar.

• • •

In July, Dannie came again for his annual summer stay at Hemlock Hill Homestead.

On the evening of his arrival, Nancy suggested to Omar and Dannie, "Let's plan a real picnic in a few weeks. It would be nice to invite Joes and Jacobs and the Fishers and Ivor and Helga.

"We could load our eats on the big flat wagon and all take a ride back to the Hemlock Hill cabin. Then we could picnic right there in the clearing. Maybe it would even suit Mamm and Daed and the whole family to come from back home, too."

"Say, that's a super idea!" Dannie said enthusiastically. "We could put a few big watermelons in the cold springs up there, and take along a big freezer full

of hand-cranked blueberry ice cream!"

Omar was all for it, too. The picnic was planned for the last Saturday in July. Nancy passed the word around and sent a letter back home. Happily, it suited the whole family to come from Whispering Brook Farm, too.

The day of the picnic was one of those rare, extra-clear, and blessedly cooler, almost fall-like days. The cornstalks in the fields were a deep green, already eight-to-ten-feet tall and still growing. The blue, blue sky above was cloudless, and the evergreens on Hemlock Hill were etched breathtakingly clear against the horizon.

By ten o'clock everyone had arrived, and the big farm wagon was loaded down with people of all sizes and various hampers of food.

"I hope we see deer," Lydia said eagerly. "I've never seen a real live fawn."

"All this noise will scare them away," Omar told her. "But you will see a wolf." He guided the stocky workhorses up the trail into the woods. "Ivor and Helga are probably there already."

"I can't wait to see the waterfall Dannie was telling me about." Susie had never been that far into the woods.

Steven, Henry, and Dannie had their fishing lines along. Nancy and Sally were toting their binoculars and hoping to see some rare birds.

Omar and Andrew said they would tag along behind the bird-watchers. Andrew claimed it was "to make sure you don't talk so much that you scare the

birds away." Omar promised "to protect you girls from wild animals, and see that you don't get lost."

It was a jolly family occasion. Everyone was chattering and trading jokes as they rode along. Even the horses seemed to be in a good mood, looking around once in a while to see what was going on.

Dannie could hardly wait to see the little old cabin again. He had spent enchanting, lonely, and bittersweet days there with Bandit. That time had proved to be the turning point in his attitudes and in the course of his life.

He remembered how crushed he had felt after his dad left him. Mom Petersheim had often told him, "There's nothing on earth that heaven can't heal. There can be a hidden blessing in even the severest trials, if we don't become bitter and hardened."

Dannie knew that she and Dad Petersheim had been praying for him and trusting in the Lord. Now he counted it a great blessing to be part of such a big, happy family.

They were entering the shadowy woods with the enormous pines sweeping overhead. Hemlock boughs were drooping gracefully to the forest floor, thickly carpeted with pine needles.

The woods and the caring family seemed to put the parts of his life together. Dannie felt his heart overflowing with happiness.

He thought Hemlock Hill was the most beautiful spot on earth, with the lively little squirrels frisking around and chattering up in the trees. Next came the refreshing springs and the beds of mint, and then the view of the scenic little cabin hideaway, surrounded by wildlife and singing birds.

A sudden idea flashed into Dannie's mind. *I know!* He could hardly keep from shouting it out loud. *Someday I'll buy Ivor's place! They are old and . . . sometime will sell it. Then I'd always be near these lovely Hemlock woods, . . . for the rest of my life!*

Dannie had no way of knowing then that he would hold this dream in his heart for another ten years before it came true.

The Author

THE author's pen name is Carrie Bender. She is a member of an old order group. With her husband and children, she lives among the Amish in Lancaster County, Pennsylvania. Her books are listed on page 2.

Bender is the popular author of the Whispering Brook Series, books about fun-loving Nancy Petersheim as she grows up surrounded by her close-knit Amish family, friends, and church community. This series is for children and a general audience.

The Miriam's Journal Series is also well appreciated by a wide reading public. These stories in journal form are about a middle-aged Amish woman who for the first time finds love leading to marriage. Miriam and Nate raise a lively family and face life with faith and faithfulness. Bender portrays their ups and downs through the seasons, year after year.

Miriam's Cookbook presents recipes for the tasty, hearty meals of Amish everyday life. They are spiced with fitting excerpts from Bender's books.

The Dora's Diary Series, also in journal form, tells about Miriam and Nate's adopted daughter going out with the young folks, becoming a schoolteacher, and growing close to a special boyfriend.

Herald Press (616 Walnut Ave., Scottdale, PA 15683) has received many fan letters for Carrie Bender. Readers say they have "thoroughly enjoyed" her "heartwarming" books. Her writing is "like a breath of fresh air," telling of "loyalty, caring, and love of family and neighbors." They give "a comforting sense of peace and purpose."

Library Journal says, "Bender's writing is sheer poetry. It leads readers to ponder the intimate relationship of people and nature."